Moonlight
into Marzipan

✳

MOONLIGHT INTO MARZIPAN

✳

Sunetra Gupta

PHOENIX HOUSE
London

First published in Great Britain in 1995 by Phoenix House,
Orion House,
5 Upper St Martin's Lane, London WC2H 9EA

Copyright © 1995 Sunetra Gupta

The right of Sunetra Gupta to be identified as
the author of this work has been asserted by her
in accordance with the Copyright, Designs
and Patents Act 1988.

The text contains the author's translations of works by Rabindranath Tagore and
Bibhuti Bhusan Banerjee

A CIP catalogue record for this book is available
from the British Library.

ISBN 1897 97676 2 HB
ISBN 1897 97677 0 PB

Photoset by Deltatype Ltd, Ellesmere Port
Printed and bound in Great Britain by
Butler & Tanner Ltd, Frome and London

To Adrian

Prologue

✳

That was a month of salt, Esha would tell us later, that was a month of petrified time, a mummified month, with each afternoon as slow crystals dissolving darkly upon her young tongue, she would wander the forest with her grandfather's rusty walking stick, stalk the small stretch of overgrown railway track, each day to revel in the mock discovery of the glorious wreck of an abandoned rail carriage, smooth with decay. And each morning she would wake to the whiteness of fierce sun, the sky a bed of dull salt, the starched clothes of her grandparents flapping mercilessly taut outside the window, and the acid smell of unformed paper building stealthily in the back yard. For though they had barbed and wired the tall wall that separated her grandfather's house from the rest of the factory compound, the strange sour smell of paperpulp would drench the back garden on windless days. There she would spend her mornings, prisoner to this small patch of walled earth, with yards of arithmetic, and a tall steel tumbler of saltsweet yoghurt. And then the maid would arrive with the coconut oil, massage her small head until her hair stood in fat spikes, the better to drag her by to the well, where buckets of earthcold water would be thrown over her defenceless flesh, salt soap lathered. Then lunch, with her grandparents in soft speckled silence, and the afternoon gathering tremulously upon her fingertips like the yolk of all her yesterdays, still unhatched.

These images, unventilated all these years, steam softly as they are dragged out from the humid recesses of my memory, they are yours, my love, my many-laundered thoughts, yours to fold and crease, and even to dye, that the patches might be hidden in the flawed remembrance of a tropical blue, the mothsmells rinsed from an angle of elbow, long forgotten, the shape of a clockhand wrenched out from its face to clean an urgent pipe.

I tell you of a child resting a grim cheek against the metal weight of an old afternoon, this is the image that returns most often to me of Esha, long before I knew her, fashioning her fate behind her young large eyes, a destiny that she would exchange with mine, I who had grown into manhood without the least trace of ambition, I would stumble into fame, and she would spill her brains into the rodent-rich trough between the underground tracks, she who had borne the myriad saddle-points in our lives with such sweet selflessness, all along.

Did she not know, could she not guess, clutching my hand on our first shopping expedition in this foreign land, five years ago, could she not feel the despair in my tenderness, did she not see that the compass of our existence had become too distended to contain our love?

The aubergines look as if someone has spent hours polishing them, she said.

We came upon an aisle of potato crisps, I touched her shoulder, should we have left Calcutta? I said, do you think we will be happy here? Of course, she said, we have worked so hard for this, of course we will be happy.

Chearsley took us out to dinner that evening, we had asparagus soup, and fried whitebait, and veal cutlets, a proper English meal to welcome you, Chearsley explained of his choice of supper, although London abounds in ethnic restaurants, he assured us, if this does not suit your palate, local anaesthetic this to some, he said waving his soup spoon, local anaesthetic, he repeated, humbly content with his own joke.

The child rests her cheek against the sunwarmed carcass of a rail carriage, grains of forest darkness slip swiftly between her small fingers, it was a month of salt, she said, and I was born of it, for the I that came and the I that left knew little of each other, separated by paperpulp, and the saltwarm stretches of my grandfather's snores, in this month of salt, my memories grew particulate, my thoughts crystalline, and the alchemy of numbers became the substance of my dreams.

And ten years later she would write her first love letter to me, on that same cane table where she had done her long division, the acid smoke of unformed paper building around her, she would remind me that I was her destiny, poor and unworthy as I was, she had locked her numberstruck soul with my impoverished genius, together we would save the world.

We married, and she came to live in our cramped flat, taught Mathematics at a local school, and came home in the evenings and made chapattis for the whole family, every evening without fail, I would watch her as she divided the dough into twenty-eight balls, four apiece for the seven of us, rolled each out in six deft strokes, and then popped them on the hotplate to rise, the regularity of her movements would stir a certain nausea in me, and yet I would watch, hypnotised by the metronomic swing of her arms.

Five years and three miscarriages later, we moved into the house where she had spent her childhood, the house that her grandfather had built on the outskirts of the city, in the style of a colonial villa, for her father left it to us in his will rather than to his son, who had never returned from across the seas, made a life in Liverpool, far far away. We lived in a mellow and solid peace, Esha and I, and her mother, a peace that I would swill in my calm mouth on evenings that we spent in shared silence, her mother knitting, she scratching at her thesis, and I in imperturbable inanimate bliss, pretending to read Russian novels. It was this period of utter inactivity that primed my being for the avalanche of ideas that were to follow. Free from the frenzy of love, of pain, of the blood that she had gushed whenever we had tried to have a child, free from the tensions of my extended family, the tangy tracklements of communal existence, hostage only to time, my battlements against the anxieties of the tropics hardened, I became a self-contained, isolated sphere of pure thought, I sold their ailing jalopy, and turned the garage into a laboratory.

It was a month of salt, she said, I would wake to the sandy strokes of the hall clock, shake my bednet free of dead moths, fold it neatly away under the mattress, crumbling coir through its seams, shards of light would pattern upon the wall, and life would seem merely a blueprint for some vastly grander scheme.

I would like to build a laboratory in the garage, I said to them, one evening. Esha ran an inky hand through her hair, it has no windows, she said.
So much the better.
What about the car? her mother asked.
That rustbucket should have been sold many years ago. It costs less to take taxis than to maintain that dinosaur.
What about the driver?
He goes with the car, I said ruthlessly.
Your cousin will get him another job, said Esha, her eyes suddenly sparkling, suddenly complicitous.
So we called in the Muslim carpenter, and gave him specifications for the benches and shelves, cupboards where we would keep our lusty organic salts, we found glassware in wholesale in College Street, I never knew whether she did this all to humour me, in apology for not having given me a child, or whether she had never stopped believing that I was a gift to her, that I must be nurtured, that one day I would turn grass into gold. A dog, with sore sad eyes, would sit outside the folding door, and watch us, we came to love him, on the day we inaugurated the laboratory, we gave him a large bowl of festive rice-pudding.

Spare us these futile digressions, pleads Yuri Sen, struggling with these coarsegrained fragments of my past that you, my love, have called upon him to render in a more civilised tongue than mine. Yuri Sen, summoned to scan the ravine between my thoughts and their unrefined transcription (as if it were not wider even than the gap that yawns between him and me), grumbles incessantly as he is presented with page upon page of unguarded recollection, fistfuls of disconnected impressions that I have churned out for you to reshape into a palatable history, a host of limbless anecdotes, for you and him to varnish and tie together into the story of my life.

Spare us these digressions, cries Yuri Sen, who wants such trivial details as the dog that you got attached to while you were building your lab.

What do you want then, all of you, hungry for scraps with which to pad the knuckles of this story, the story of my success, and her failures, and the failure of the architecture of numbers to sustain the universe, what more do you want other than thin muscles of dramatically dispensable detail?

Do you know, asks Yuri Sen, how mice steal eggs?

Grass became gold, or rather gold became grass, but not for many winters, and then it was copper that did it, the small earstud that accidentally fell into the potion, and gave vital catalysis to the mysterious process, we had made food from light, and still she rolled dough in the kitchen in the evenings, soaked lentils in moonbeams, made cottage cheese boats with cashewnut sails.

Mice, says Yuri Sen, steal eggs in pairs – pairs of mice, that is, not pairs of eggs – one will lie flat on its back, clutching the egg with its paws against the cushion of its belly, while the other takes its tail and drags his partner back to the nest.

· 7 ·

I was not aware, I answer, that mice had any use for eggs? What on earth would they do with them?

Cheese omelettes, no doubt, replies Yuri Sen.

Gold became grass, light folded neatly into small tasty morsels before our eyes at the insistence of a a few grains of tarnished copper, and then there were months of pain, devoted to the articulation of this fact, months of anguish, when Esha would sit with the dogeared thesaurus, and tease out a respectable grammar for the alchemical routine, and in the kitchen her mother devised recipes for our slime, if people are to eat this, she said, it cannot taste like pondscum, her mother said, throwing a fistful of ground coriander into the works.

And then the words began suddenly to regiment themselves around our ideas, to reveal and conceal in the right proportions the fantasy we had made real, how her copper earring slipping from earlobe into the cold mass had made it seethe and spit and weave grass from light, we had poached on the territories of creation, what nascent syllables could dignify our fearful act?

Spare us these impoverished symmetries, begs Yuri Sen, we are here to record the story of your life, not to chart your colourless fantasies.

Can this be the sole purpose though of his dark presence, I wonder, for the stingy conclusion of this tale is now in sight, what was to have been a big bang is fast ending in a whimper, my benefactor's patience is wearing thin, and perhaps it is to supervise my dismissal rather than to translate my perverse scribbles, that Sir Percival Partridge has stationed him in my apartment, his pocket Narcissus, Yuri Sen. For weeks now he has been sharing my incommodious apartment, the devil's own apprentice, Yuri Sen, besmirching this unchristened space that I still call my own, though my tenure is rapidly trickling away, my five years are almost up, and I have failed to repeat my miracles. I believe my benefactor's patience would have run out long ago if this had not all been a whim – a flight of fancy more than a rational investment – to bring me to this land and give me the chance to work my magic on a grander scale, to give the opportunities that I never had in my Calcutta garage, if this had not been just another of his lunatic projects, the infamous Sir Percival Partridge would have booted me out of here long ago, I suspect.

He had arrived one morning with his bags, Yuri Sen, complaining bitterly about the new growth of bookshops on the High Street.

The whole city will soon be one large second-hand book market, he said, unlacing his gloves. I saw at least five new clearing houses during the cab ride, whatever happened to the Ginseng Parlour? the Behala Brasserie? the permanently bankrupt Futon Centre?

They've all been taken over by the discount book dealers, I'm afraid, I confirmed. It was true, I had seen it happen, before my very eyes. And not just this corner, all of London, it would seem, was buckling under this giant conspiracy, the insidious growth of bargain bookshops, even the derelict steak-and-kidney pie place under the railway bridge had been appropriated, I had noticed the grimy glass now hid smutty photography manuals and wafer-thin hardcovers on Impressionist artists, all with blue before and after tags, jauntily obscuring part of the title. Within a week of Yuri Sen's arrival, two other bookshops had sprung up under our very noses, replacing the Chinese bakery by the post office, and the bookmaker's across the road. The young heterodox is determined, however, to undermine this vicious intrigue. As a first step he is monitoring the epidemic, keeping careful records in a small leatherbound notebook, in the evenings he fiddles with the figures and clucks away at his computer, the youth has a degree in Statistics, it seems, that he acquired in Shantiniketan, at Tagore's idyllic university, which explains, I suppose, his conversance with the poet's work.

Yuri Sen, so named for the man who circled the earth in the year of his birth, I will call him Yuri, his father had declared, Dr Sen of Dagenham, clipping the defunct lifeline of his newborn son, I will call him Yuri, so that he too may one day achieve dominion over the skies. His other children he called Luna and Sputnik, for reasons of theme, I believe, rather than predestiny.

Yuri Sen, then, began life burdened already with cosmic ideals, he spun through childhood in cardboard space helmets, faltered into adolescence with a crippling vacuum upon his lips, and instead of boldly going where no man had gone before, walked back in his father's footsteps to Bengal, returned holy in his anticipation of an ordinary life, and then before he knew it, this hapless specimen of the Bengali race, that the nineteenth century would have seen silkshod in poetry parlours, this petty Adonis, who might fifty years ago have blown his soft brains out across the feet of a passing Viceroy, instead was sucked into the mirrored halls of Sir Percival's home, when for seven long years he has lived above an aviary, upon floors of glass – sometimes we eat there, when the fancy seizes Sir Percival, birds flying unnervingly beneath our feet. He is not pleased at his temporary expulsion from this peculiar haven, Yuri Sen, and even less so at being forced to wander the meagre valleys of my past, it's not as if any of this interests me, he snarls, surveying my volatile scribbles, at least if there were something to read between the lines, he complains, chewing upon his pen.

And so he reluctantly learns, Yuri Sen, that of my childhood memories the first that has any shape or taste is the death of the boy across the road, who like me was called Promothesh, and even nicknamed, like myself, Pappa. For three winter months I saw him wither, every afternoon I would watch him from my bed, where I lay with my mother, feigning sleep, as he sat on the narrow verandah to syrup his wasting limbs in the winter sunlight.

(Spare me this luxuriance, cries Yuri Sen, your prose is like a female orgasm, many-layered and formless – give the mica of ejaculatory exposition, remember you are a man, says Yuri Sen, though the Poet would have cheerfully had you all in a state of perpetual androgyny, would he not?)

I watched him die, the boy with my name, my face even, for at that age, it was easy to see our unhardened features in each other, our eyes undistinguished by our histories, unformed yet, destiny was still ahead then and not behind.

(What you are trying to say then, is that your features were like putty, waiting to be moulded by your realities – and your eyes, your eyes were limpid pools, organs of pure sight, that with time would become your most treasured instruments of love?

Shut up, Yuri Sen, hold your tongue and let me writhe.)

He would sit upon the balcony in the thick twilight, listening over and over to his favourite record:

> The day ends, in the land of sleep the same phantom
> And on the other shore, amid the golden corn
> The same spirit sings her distracting song –
> Oh come, those who would take this last boat with me
>   across the river.

It was the very last verse that was the most eerie, I would stand, washing drainslime off the much battered deuce ball at the creaky tubewell, and shiver as these last few strains sifted slowly through the darkness toward me:

> He, who has not been blessed with the burden of flowers
> He, whose crops have failed yet again
> He, who can only laugh at his own tears
> He, for whom when the day is over, no light comes to relieve
>   the dark
> It is he who sits in the shadows of the shore listening to her
>   song.

And in the dining room, my mother would be waiting with whey and puffed rice that, in my hurry to be out on the streets with the boys, I had neglected to finish. Wash your hands, she would command softly, her eyes bright with tears, why not he rather than the neighbour's son, she surely wondered, what chord of steel separated our destinies, that he, with my name, and my face, should waste away into the tropical silence, while I, I would thrive, would grow to manhood, and earn my keep as purveyor of promiscuous peptides, and I, rather than he, would one day, in a small South Calcutta garage, stumble upon the sternest secrets of life, why should his story fill one meagre paragraph, and mine more than can hold between these wide covers.

The room fills with the sound of ripping paper, you look up and bite your lovely lips, silently fingering your robust tresses, sandstrewn about the brocade cushions. You watch the afternoon light snake across my unweeded pate and lose itself upon the coarse weave of my woollen waistcoat, in the vulgar intrusions of blue upon yellow – Esha's favourite colours, once. I reach for the silver merry-go-round of those turpentines and oils that dignify, at your insistence, our lunch sandwiches, take knife to mustard, smear a little upon my tongue. Brave spinach and prawn have earlier submitted to the inglorious dissemblage beneath the onslaught of my impatient enzymes, and now, stripped of their identities, await assimilation, ruthlessly decoded, strange how sometimes our metaphors mingle, yours and mine, laying bare the most elemental roots of thought, your texts and my complex carbohydrates, eggs of the same basket?

And which basket is that? I ask you, kissing champagne bubbles off your firm lips, will they not break, crammed all in one basket, these eggs?

The better to make omelettes from, you answer, between the meanderings of my thick tongue.

And later, sadly certain that this penultimate act of love

would also find its place between these covers, I watched you sleep, and held my thoughts, safe this once from you, close to my lips, blew them one by one into the soft night, smelt my armpits for signs of disaster, and resolved to express myself, the following day, in a language that we did not share, my mother tongue. Tomorrow, I would bewilder you with page upon page of inscrutable hieroglyph, and so claim some part of my ego as surely my own. And there I was wrong, for you only laughed and declared it a marvellous idea, that I should encode my memories in this easier script rather than my laboured English, you smiled and summoned that bilingual catamite to decipher my scrawlings, my flights of native fancy, guarded by fat strokes of watery mustard, you got on the telephone to Sir Percival Partridge, and requested the services of Yuri Sen.

Memories, says Yuri Sen, must be stored within clean and dry spaces, where the light is clear and even – though not bright enough to dazzle. Whereas you, he tells me, have either crammed them into the dampest recesses of your mind or left them to bake in the heat of your newest lust.

Memories, says Yuri Sen, must be kept covered lest they be streaked with the porphyry of emotion, so Matteo Ricci warned the Chinese. And on no account should memories be suspended from a pulley or balanced on a beam, for then the slightest wind might cause them to fall and crumble, or to sway in ceaseless ideographic turmoil . . .

My cheek catches the frantic spray of a wet birdwing, a grimy sparrow has flown in through the window and landed upon the desk, soon it will fling its small life back into the deep curtain of rain, leaving the damp cat hungry and uncertain of its wits, I take comfort in these small creatures that surround me, that have no place in my autobiography, and I insist on recording their handsome unease. You will no doubt drive a pen through their trivial antics, mercilessly plough this muddy page, still warm from my thoughts, for no tale is ever the worse for its retelling, you insist, nor any identity ever the weaker for its exchange, the story of my life cannot possibly suffer in your precious hands, you assure me, much as you might embellish each blemish, scar deeper the salt white, soaked by my useless tears.

My head froths with the dead eye white of an unpupilled evening, stiff myrrh maids circling the room with glasses of sherry, English summer creeping about their faces. The teenage sons of Chearsley and Cuddington, solicitors to Sir Percival, dispense alcohol and silence, in unmistakably Hibernian quantities, chuckling quietly to themselves behind white-topped tables – BOYS!! – Partridge roars – BE QUIET – he clears his throat and begins: We are gathered today to honour the memory of my father Archibald Partridge . . .

The sons of Chearsley and Cuddington have upset a jarful of ladybirds onto the table, they crawl between the tumblers in dazed disapproval of their new surrounds. They are your ladybirds, I think, Esha whispered to me. I groaned, and made my way across to the table, damn you, I said to the boys, that's six months' worth of work down the drain, your fathers will not be pleased. Chearsley Jr shrugged, but a small slippery shadow of fear erupted over the young Cuddington's smug features, Cuddington Sr I surmised was a tougher parent than Chearsley Sr, Chearsley I remembered had lost his wife when the child was small, and besides there could be no doubt, Chearsley was the weaker of the two. Your father will not be pleased, I said darkly to Chearsley Jr, as he slowly and deliberately crushed a confused insect under a highball glass, smiling mercilessly.

Fuck my father, said Chearsley Jr.

Not for anything in this world, said Yuri Sen gloomily, who had crept up behind me to watch the fun.

It was Yuri Sen's idea that we go on to a jazz club after the dinner, the Quadrupeds are on at the F—, he mentioned with characteristic casualness, as if pulling silk out of his mouth.

The Quadrupeds, said Esha wistfully, they were playing at the F— on our first night in London, Chearsley took us to see them, on our first night in London.

Then we must go, said Yuri Sen, almost tenderly, unless you found them insufferable?

No, no, replied my wife, it somehow makes sense that I should see them tonight.

Only because like all of them, you are addicted to coincidence, thought Yuri Sen. Six hours later she would throw herself in front of a tube train, but this, like most of the future, we did not know then.

And you, the late light bronze upon your hair, you, flicking a stray ladybird off your marble wrist, you, before my breath could ever have softened the parting of your lips, you smiled, and admitted utter ignorance of the artistry of the Quadrupeds. I wanted to touch you more than I had ever wanted to touch you before, I wanted to run my bruised tongue over the enrheumed marble of your lips, so bravely locked in smile, to run my heavy tongue between the rivulets of your small laughter, I closed my lustworn eyes and took a step back, and came down rather heavily upon Chearsley Jr's toes.

You bastard, the Chearsley boy yelled, you elephant-footed creep, you've just destroyed my left foot.

Come now, said Chearsley Sr, who had rushed across the room upon hearing the pup yelp, that's no way to talk to anybody. He looked pleadingly up at his son, with those mouse eyes of his that had appeared, dull behind the steam of his saltless perspiration, those leaky grey eyes that had met mine, one steaming afternoon, many years ago, this is the correct address? he had inquired timidly, hell of a job finding the place, he said, mopping the beadlets off his brow, Charles Chearsley, at your service, I represent the Partridge Trust.

Esha had given him tea, sad saucerfuls he drank, poured from his cup – I can only drink it lukewarm, he told us, but not cold, cold like it gets if you leave it in the cup to cool – Charles

Chearsley, teastains spreading up his cheesecloth sleeves, like an unwary chromatograph.

(*What? asks Yuri Sen, chromatograph?*

. *It's an instrument, I begin to explain wearily, an instrument . . .*

Oh, that chromatograph, Yuri Sen interrupts, I didn't recognise it in the Bengali.)

You have your laboratory in the garage? Chearsley had inquired incredulously, shakily resetting his cup upon his much maltreated saucer, you have done all this work in your garage?

We haven't been able to afford a private car in a long time, my wife said graciously, so why not? What better use for the garage?

What better use for a garage? she said to Yuri Sen, two weeks before she died, struggling through our strange tale on Sir Percival's request.

We were walking on the grounds of the Partridge estate, it was a soft summer afternoon, and every sweet flower scent stuck in her throat, as Esha told our story, her gaze darting between you and me like a badly broken thread.

You should write your autobiography, said Sir Percival to me, it would be throcking good publicity for the Trust.

I'm afraid my English is a little limited for that, I replied.

Partridge waved aside the paper webs of my modesty with characteristic delicacy, of course, you wouldn't have to write the bloody thing, he said, leave that part of it to her, he gestured towards you.

Leave the writing to her, said Partridge, throwing the remains of his sandwich to a passing peacock, leave the writing to Alexandra Vorobyova, your task is merely to harness her fancies with the morality of narrative, to limit the profligacies of the twice-filtered image.

Twice filtered, yes, once through the coarse grain of my memory, and then through the fine meshes of your prose, and to this I have added other layers, for I have chosen to transcribe my fondest thoughts in my own rainsodden language, territory only to Yuri Sen's incurious probings, must you use so many complex consonants, he yawns, Yuri Sen, bored beyond belief by the sorry joints of my preposterous fate.

On the day that she died Esha bought herself a large tub of Dutch Double Chocolate icecream, I came home to find her deep within it, dark smears upon her eyebrows, and I sat down beside her with my guilt heavy as an unborn tumour slinging against my gut. I thought I deserved this, she said, her mouth bleeding icecream, I thought I would pamper myself, she told me.

It is a Western notion, is it not, she continued, that physical comforts can serve as antidote for pain, that a warm herbal bath can smooth all but the deepest of anguish, and even that, for then there is the scented water to fill your aching nostrils with the bliss of drowning.

We must dress, I said wearily, for the dinner at the Trust.

So we must, she said, I have shaken out my South Indian silk, but I was not sure how you wanted go . . .

I am alright as I am, I said sadly. And so she wrapped herself in the ambivalent blue of a peacock's neck, stabbed her ears with emeralds, and rustled with me into the gilt boardroom, where the sons of Chearsley and Cuddington were busily dispensing alcohol and silence – in unmistakably Hibernian quantities, you said smiling, appearing at my elbow, bordered in the blackness of my desire.

It was Yuri Sen's idea that we go to a jazz club after dinner, to see the Quadrupeds, the inimitable brass quartet, the club was packed, I stood by you in hot and holy stupor, swaying against your warmth, my fists clenched, my eyes closed, I barely noticed when Esha touched my wrist, I'll be back in a minute, she said.

And then there was a space of no event, only the still

concentration of my desire, insulated by the groans of the saxophone, there was mass, and no motion, there was energy, without gradient, there was a coagulation in the cosmic soup.

And then there were the twin shadows of Cuddington and Chearsley, advising silence, as they led us out from within the crowd, make no statements, they warned, refuse comment, why what had happened? your wife, they told me, has thrown herself in front of a train.

Is she alright? I asked stupidly.

Let's put it this way, said Cuddington, never a man to cushion his prose, let's put it this way, she's created a major glut in the burgermeat market for sewer rats.

He sat down heavily upon the pavement, mouth bubbling blood, for Yuri Sen had just socked him in the jaw, her brains, he continued through broken teeth, her brains are wall-papering Old Street Station, you impervious bastards, couldn't you see she wasn't just walking out to take the night air.

And my first thought, my very first thought, was not of her, but of whether our passion could accommodate this absurdity, whether her monstrous act would not lodge like a fishbone between the membranes of our lust, would you forgive me, I wondered, if the depth of my remorse did not overshadow my passion? would you forgive me the shape of my loss, if it did not fill the cleft of my being? if my senses were not all consumed by the spectre of her death, but some dripped over in relief towards you, could you forgive me?

Let me never rest my head again upon a shoulder that does not quiver but a little under a patina of untruths, let my palate never be soothed but by the grazings of tongues thick with secrets, let my lust never be quickened but by the sheen of lies upon trembling eyes. Integrity, my love, is purely a personal vice.

Hardly so, you retort, integrity is an illusion, a Narcissan flattery, as if the man in the mirror were more you than anyone else.

And is he not? He moves as I do, speaks with the same hesitation, and when I leave, he appears to oblige.

How do you know? you whisper hot upon my ear, and he, in the mirror, trembles as I do, under the false weight of the image of your lips. You continue: how do you know that he leaves when you do, that he does not linger in his thin cage, his borrowed smile sad upon his unfulfilled features, how do you know he does not dread your return, with a few more grey hairs to soften the iron of his youth, another few lines to crowd about his eyes, how do you know that he is not there always, and that he does not hate you?

How would I know, indeed? For I have not delved into the depths of my soul as you have, you who were charged with the duty of telling my tale, who would have thought you would tire so soon of this burden, that you would journey deeper within me than I had ever been, and then disappear into the desert without telling the world what you had seen.

The Book
of Iron

✳

He kneels, his head bowed, among a pile of dead leaves at the bottom of the empty swimming pool. Wet whispers of our feet reach his proud ears and still he will not raise his eyes, our voices vein thinly through his thoughts, he will not lift his dark eyes to us. We stand at the edge of the deep end, Gorrion, for God's sake, shouts Sir Percival, crawl out of the tub and meet my friends.

Juan Gorrion, brushing leafgrains from his tweed jacket, rises to face us, the young darkness runs eagerly into the sharp hollows of his features, while we stand defined by the dying sun, he, inscrutable, scrutinises, and the darkness is measured out into the thin cracks of his cheeks by the spreading sarcasm of his smile. Juan Gorrion, gentleman and scholar, smiles and nods his noble head, it is very beautiful down here, he says in gravelly New England tones, why don't you all join me?

He steps forward and offers you his hand, now you can see the mountain blue of his eyes, your feet are bleeding badly within your glass slippers, still you brave the rungs, tweeded arms tightening about your waist. Later I will find those shoes, upturned on poolside cement, their cruel heels thick with impaled leaves. For the moment I join you, with a small cowardly leap into the shallow end, Yuri Sen follows suit, lowering himself lightly into the basin.

Gorrion's arm is thick against yours, rubbing night into the whiteness of your bare flesh, his elbow is a sharp accordion note of desire, pining mercilessly into your sweet flesh. I stand helplessly behind you, dare only to let my feeble fingers fall upon your shoulder, and you transmute this agonised movement into a seemingly paternal gesture with a small affectionate pat of your hand, your hand pats and at the same time brushes away, above us the sky is an excruciating blue.

Gorrion will take you where the grass grows wild beneath his dreams, he will fashion a journey through the basketweave of his unspeakable fantasies, and then he will disappear, without a word he will vanish, walk swiftly into the trees. All this he knows already, laying his long cheek against the pool wall, and catching the small perspiration of the new evening upon the dark curve of his lips, he pulls you to him and says, look at the stars, I had a dream, he says, last night, that I had stars in my eyes, only they were sharp-edged and cruel as salt, and made my eyes bleed, I longed for someone to lick them away, he said, Juan Gorrion, man of a thousand lies, confectioner of delectable untruths.

I need a drink, says Percival Partridge, still perched on the edge of the empty pool, I desperately need a drink.

There's some cold vodka in the pavilion, says Yuri Sen.

I'd love some vodka, says Juan Gorrion.

Will you give me a hand? asks Yuri Sen wickedly. I follow him silently out of the pool, walk across the grass to the pavilion, we climb the mossy stairs. Your daughter is sitting by the door to the changing room, staring into the growing gloom, the radio spitting softly beside her, *no one knows what it's like to be the bad man, to be the sad man, behind blue eyes*, I know the song, I say, the young man next door to us in Calcutta would play it all the time.

It is an old song, she says wearily.

Could you wash out these tumblers? asks Yuri Sen.

With pleasure, I reply, removing a pile of wet tennis towels from the marble sink. I knew the song, the boy next door would play it over and over again on his rusty machine, it was the summer that my niece was born, my brother's daughter, grown now into girlhood, the slender child that I left behind five years ago, will she recognise me when I return, if I return, and why should I not return I wonder, to play out the rest of this muddy scheme under the sad skies that spawned me, the city is much changed they tell me, but never quite how changed, do the same dungwet silences cling to the cracked alleyways? I long to ask, is the autumn wind still ripe with a poet's desire? do the tears of old vultures still wet the cheeks of night?

(*Why distract the reader with such unnecessary rhapsody, asks Yuri Sen, this is an evening of pure pain for you, it is the night that you lost her, your lover, your scribe, your soul, lost her to that cheerless puppetmaker, Professor of Politics, Juan Gorrion, man of many talents.*

What other antidote for pain, Yuri, than distraction?

If only you would let pain nourish rather than poison, says Yuri Sen, it might even become an addiction.

Heaven forbid, Yuri Sen.)

He makes puppets, says your daughter as I give her the glasses to wipe, he makes puppets as a hobby.

Who?

That man, she says, the man in the pool. She had bumped into him in the woods that afternoon, he was sitting on a stump carving marionettes' limbs from twigs, who are you, he had asked her.

I am Anya, she had replied.

That's a cute name.

You're American, she had retorted.

Hardly. I only teach here.

What do you teach?

Politics.

What kind?

Perverse.

And puppetry?

A mere avocation.

Later, she had seen him crouched at the bottom of the pool, your daughter tells me. I stopped and waited for him to look up, she says, but he never did.

Yuri Sen hands me a tray of parrot-shaped ice-cubes. We return to the pool, and descend, rather more carefully into the depths. Gorrion has lent you his jacket, you stand wonderfully misshapen at his side, it strikes me that he is your destiny, he is the man whose number you would dial by mistake when your life seemed in perfect order, he is the man selling the piano you choose to buy as a surprise for your husband, he is the stranger who takes shelter with you in the bus-stand the day before your wedding, he is the straw already sewn onto the camel's back, you could not help but follow him, as you did, into the intoxications of nowhere, I do not blame you for this, never think that I blame you for this.

Before she took her own life, Esha telephoned someone, seven random digits, and to the voice that answered she told of her gruesome intention, I am doing this to become a recurring nightmare, she said, and yet, I suspect I will only become a tender fragment of memory. But to you, unknown one, I will remain a nightmare, a black enigma, and this is some small comfort. By the time you digest this, by the time your hands stop shaking, I will have been thoroughly pulverised. Think about it, you can do nothing to stop me.

She gave her story to the newspapers, the old woman in the orange cardigan, whose number my wife had dialled, the last person she ever spoke to, who caught her words between whiffs of burning sausage, her dinner fretting upon the stove. You went to see her, many months later, you went to see her, with your notebook and pen, in her Paddington council flat, the lift only stopped on alternate floors, you had to climb down from the top floor to reach her apartment, you took her some jam tarts which she ate with great relish, it wus a strange acksint, she said, I cud barely make out wot she sed, just reelized she wus about to killerself poor thing. The fluorescent jam trickled thinly down her chin onto her orange sweater, you pulled a tissue out from your bag and gave it to her, thanks luv, nice of you to drop by, I can't hardly go out, see, because I'm no good anymore with stairs, and they won't move me to an even-numbered floor, even though I can barely walk down those stairs, did you know 'er then, the girl, shame it wus she reelly jumped, I thought she wus pulling my leg you know, and sumtimes when you tell sumone you will, you don't, if you see what I mean, luv, wus she a friend of yours, then?

I knew her, you said, I'm writing a book about her husband.

Am I to be in a book, then? she asked, that's sumthing, I can tell my daughter that when she comes on Wensday, won't believe me of course, wot sort of a book is it, then?

It's an autobiography.

Will it 'ave pictures? she asked.

Yuri Sen breaks the ice into the vodka, bloody unwieldly cubes, he says accusingly to Partridge. The lights come on in the pavilion, and a desperate cold gathers suddenly in the pit of the pool, I take Partridge his drink, and climb up to sit beside him.

Gorrion was one of my undergraduates at Oxford, he says. Gravitated soon enough across the Atlantic. One of my brightest students ever, says Sir Percival Partridge.

We had heard him arrive the night before, while dining in Yuri Sen's strange apartments, a delicious supper cunningly put together by your daughter from the leftovers of an extravagant luncheon, we were well into our prawn and parsnip soup when we heard a car draw up on the crunchy gravel, that will be Juan Gorrion, confessed Percival Partridge.

Is he joining us for dinner? you asked.

Not Gorrion, Partridge replied, he won't want to see anyone before lunchtime tomorrow, I should expect.

For a while we sat in a strange trance, listening for the slam of the car door, the scrape of suitcases against the butler's trousers, footsteps upon nightcooled marble, fading to a white silence, Yuri Sen raked the glass tabletop with his fork, and nervously quoted Tagore – *wingbeat of the wandering bird that fissures this darkness, shall I sing to your tune* – candlelight lacquered the morsel of lamb that Partridge lifted to his lips, this is throcking good! he declared, my dear, you cook far better than your mother, he said to your daughter, glowing in virginal white beside you, canaries fluttering soundlessly beneath her bare toes.

. . . or will it be the shrunken pain of curtained love that shapes my music this evening? the catamite continued, in his bastard Bengali, tilting back his chair to wipe his hands on the heavy chintz drapes that girded the windowless room. Will you translate? your daughter asked. I don't think so, he said gracefully, and raising his eyes to the glass ceiling, remarked, the stars are bright tonight, and then fell immediately to humming a popular tune from the early seventies.

The girl coloured a little, don't mind him, Partridge apologised, he's always deliciously rude.

I suspect, I offered maliciously, that he is not entirely sure what the words mean.

The catamite snorted, it's just that I object to translation on moral grounds, he said, as if it was not for the express purpose of translating my perverse scribbles that he had been sharing on weekdays my small Bayswater flat, helping you, my love, to etch my past upon the flatness of my predicament, the devil's own cartographer, Yuri Sen.

She is writing your autobiography? asks Gorrion of me, laughing in the wide dark, can you not trust yourself to talk of your life?

But to talk of oneself, Partridge reminds him, to talk of oneself is a feast that starves the guest: so said Menander. You, yourself, Gorrion, wrote an essay of that name, some thirty years ago.

Nonsense, says Yuri Sen. The feast that starves the guest is a sautéed giraffe neck on a long silver platter, twelve brothers eating with gusto, six on either side of the table.

But a feast that starves must be a feast of air, you say urgently. You offer us, already impaled upon embroidery frame, your image of the feast that starves the guest, and it is a feast of air, with delicious flavours and colours, but no substance.

A feast of the imagination? I ask, but this is taken by the rest as a new thread of inquiry.

Not bad, says Gorrion, close enough.

I could tell a story that might have had such a title, I continue. Two cunning sages, Illyol and Batapi, would turn themselves into lambs, suffer to be cooked and fed to the guests of their master, and then emerge intact from within the guests' bellies at their master's call. The exploded guests would then be divested of their possessions and hastily disposed of, all except the last, whose rare juices had digested dear Illyol and Batapi to beyond a point of no return . . .

We are talking of a feast that starves the guest, says Yuri Sen, not one that kills them.

To kill your guests, says Juan Gorrion, is far easier than to starve them.

Speak for yourself, says Yuri Sen.

And yet, at the end of the day, it is I who tell my tale rather than you, Alexandra Vorobyova, for you had tired too soon of gravying my life with your prose, and left in search of sturdier nourishment in the arms of the unknown. We sat and waited in the cold hallway of my Bayswater flat for days for you to return, your daughter's belly swelling with Yuri Sen's child. We waited, your daughter, creation of your flesh, and I, creation of your frivolous intellect, we waited for you to return. Yuri Sen lugged home the shopping, cooked us dull meals, wired Sir Percival for money, and refused to look into an abortion for the girl, life is sacred, he declared, all the more so when it is accidental.

And what possessed you, in the first place, to slake your small curiosities upon this innocent girl's flesh, Yuri Sen?

It was the quality of the night, he will reply, the mist that descended into the caverns of the swimming pool, softening the stars. You all climbed out one by one, Sir Percival – aching for a violin sonata, Alexandra and Juan Gorrion – aching to make love, you following them like a dejected pup. I put my shawl across Anya's trembling shoulders, raised my vodka glass to her lips, washed them with the palest of fires, and then, without reason, pressed my own cold lips upon hers, felt the sharp edge that divides disgust from desire cutting keen into my loins, she dropped to her knees among the sodden leaves in numb rapture, pulled me down with her, and then, like the smashing of a precious china service, it was over, mercifully over. I got up and began to walk away, feeling no remorse, no release, not even the faintest trickle of relief. But I did not go, I circled the pool floor a few times, and then returned to where she lay, her thin thighs pressed together, I lifted her head gently onto my lap, stroked her warm cheeks. She took my hand and put it on a pale proud breast, my fingers stiffened, I marched them softly back to the neutral territory of her neck, smoothed away damp strands of hair. We sat long together in silence, until the night hardened, and the stars came rushing again into adamant focus, that is how it happened, said Yuri Sen, and my blind seed, scenting perhaps that this was their only chance, and pampered by the unfamiliarity of her blood, found their quivering quarry.

What an evening it was then, with you and Gorrion entwined in the tentacles of your manic conversations, proud with rich lust, sunk deep in dread leather, sipping Peruvian liquor. You and Gorrion lacquering your eager tongues with Pisco Sour, and I, among the inflamed tapestries, with toast and marmalade. Behind thick glass, Sir Percival could be heard sobbing in alcohol-swollen grief, and Yuri Sen, the devil take him, was ravishing your daughter, our sweet angel, Anya, on the cold floor of the mist-filled pool.

I stood alone, in the long hall, for a long time, scrutinising the tapestries, munching through a pile of thickly marmaladen toast, I noticed that the bland motheaten scapes concealed a wealth of absurd detail: many-headed men melting books of brass, hollow-wombed serpents swelling with glandous wine, a stork awaiting decapitation by a strange crisscrossing of sticks, but not all of the world's imagination could soothe me then. I took my plate down into the cavernous kitchen, and there sat in the glow of the refrigerator, my head upon the wooden table, numb beyond bitterness, wondering: should I follow if you flee?

Your daughter's head upon his thigh, Yuri Sen sat, enchained by his dreadful act of tenderness. Anya slept a desperate sleep, her senses sulphured by his growing disgust. Yuri Sen reached into his pocket and took out a pair of paper wings, unfolded them over the sleeping girl; we had been that afternoon to a costume luncheon in a nearby village, you as Cinderella, Yuri Sen as a winged beast, Sir Percival as myself and I as Sir Percival, I still wore his waistcoat and watch chain, his trousers still gathered with several safety-pins about my waist. Gorrion had not yet emerged from his room when we left, would he have accompanied us, I wondered, what would he have come as, what disguise could he have adopted, a man of so many masks, Juan Gorrion?

I sat in the nerveless dark of the kitchen, and remembered how it was here that I had first ever set eyes upon you, crouched upon the flagstones, behind a pile of hardboiled eggs, your fingers blue from eggpeeling, your hair coppery with onion-sweat. We are terribly short of hands here, you pleaded, can you help?

This man, my dear, said Sir Percival to you, this man is helping us fashion the very substance of life, you cannot ask him to spend his few moments of leisure peeling eggs.

Someone will certainly have to help, you answered, if you want the hordes to be fed.

It was the day of the annual Partridge Spring Picnic, the grounds were crawling with hungry and privileged men and women.

But he, said Sir Percival, thumping me on the back, he will soon make a way to feed millions, this man, I assure you, my dear Alexandra Vorobyova, will restore Eden to earth, reverse the Fall, throw manna to heaven, you cannot ask him to peel eggs.

Will you? you asked.

With pleasure, I replied, kneeling down beside you, my palms pricking with an amused desire.

It was the sin of knowledge that got us thrown out of Eden, said Percival Partridge, and it is knowledge that will lead us back in.

Anya dreamt of dwarves, chipping away within her with little pickaxes, to carve a cavity that they could stuff with small gems, she lay upon Yuri Sen's lap, his cold seed swaying within her, and dreamt of dwarves.

Not here, you said to Juan Gorrion, not here, you said as his hand scorpioned upon your thigh, where then? he laughed, his lips globed with blood, I would take you upon a bed of stars, he said, I would have you in a funnel of time, rushing backwards, said Juan Gorrion, if I were my Maker, I would make love to you in a loop of infinity, but I am a man, said Juan Gorrion, and I am going to fuck your brains out on this sofa.

Anya dreamt of a whole race of dwarves, streaming in and out of her, forging within her the uncreated landscapes of their dreams, until her fluted flesh rose in wrath against them, and with her head upon Yuri Sen's lap, Anya groaned and muttered their oblivion.

I must have fallen asleep where I sat, for I woke with my head buried in my arms, on the kitchen table, I woke and saw a small pair of legs struggling in the pantry window, kicking against the jars of pickles and preserves, a small pair of feet, sockless but shod. I rose and walked, half in dream, through the open pantry door, towards the narrow aperture that held this grubby half portion of boy. I held him by the waist and gently pulled, until hungry stomach, birdribbed chest, freckled neck, one by one emerged, and finally, a frightened face. He ran immediately from my arms, hardly before I had set him down, he ran out of the pantry and full tilt into the butler, Blake, who had come down to the kitchen for his breakfast. Blake gave the child a loathful look and pushed him away, settled down to his cornflakes, started a little when I walked out of the pantry, who was that child? I asked.

One of them refugee brats, it'll be, answered Blake. And then, in a brighter tone: you're up early, sir, can I get you some tea?

What refugee brats? I asked, perplexed.

Oh, don't you know, you said, appearing suddenly, liquidly sated, at the door, don't you know? you asked, dripping a dense and alcoholic satisfaction. Did I not know that these were the orphans that Sir Percival was fighting to keep in this country, two hundred children, orphaned by war, they were to be sent back to their burning lands, Sir Percival was struggling to prevent this, he had just won a reprieve of a week from the Home Office, on the condition that he would keep them and feed them, while they made their final decision. So there we were, two hundred orphans, for the week – we must stay and help, you announced, we really must stay and help.

There was a time when Esha spent her Saturday mornings giving free tuition to a few slum children. I would return from morning rehearsals (for that was when I was still active in the college Drama Society) to find her perched upon the low verandah wall, the ragged children at her feet, listening as she explained to them the mystery of numbers, how numbers too could think and feel, how numbers had resolved to hold up the universe, when all else failed, the pain of primality would purify the world. You must see the beauty of numbers, she would urge them, the gaping children, their faces overshined for this adventure, you must learn to love numbers, she would tell them, not as a miser loves numbers, but as a poet loves the clouds for the million shapes they can take. You must love numbers, for God has designed the universe out of numbers, you must revere numbers, she told them, the goggle-eyed slum children, whose scabied feet her mother would not allow into the house. Perhaps I can turn the garage into a schoolroom, she said once, as ever bursting with ideas.

Two hundred orphans, waiting to be fed. We scrubbed out the bathtubs and stirred porridge within them, bags of instant oatmeal, and cauldrons of boiling milk. Blake was sent into town for sugar, and four hundred sausages, and cartons of instant potato mash. I sat at the edge of the tub with a ladle, slopping out porridge into hungry bowls, until it lay only half an inch thick, but then a few urchins jumped in and licked the tub clean. Stay in there, commanded Juan Gorrion, you need a good wash, just drop your clothes outside. And two hundred children were bathed, and made to huddle under blankets while Blake went back into town to fetch two hundred track suits in various sizes, and several multiples of that in under-garments and socks. Yuri Sen had worked out a statistical distribution for size, and it was by these probabilities that Blake was to structure his shopping. At the end of it, there were a handful of children left without clothes their size, but no more, claimed Yuri Sen with a shrug, than might have been from natural error, had we painstakingly documented individual sizes. No matter how you looked at it: the forest would always obscure the trees, pronounced Yuri Sen.

The children stayed for two weeks, swarming about the house and grounds, blissfully unaware of their impending expulsion from this Eden. What will happen to them when they return? I asked Juan Gorrion, this we cannot tell, he replied, but we fear the worst.

If they go, said Juan Gorrion, drawing deeply on his cigarette, if they go, I will go with them.

Two hundred children, gambolling happily on the lawns, the skies swaying with their small laughter, their slight tears, and I, like the Selfish Giant, imprisoned in my pain, buried in the dark gloom of the leathered library, I wrote and wrote, but you had no time to transcribe my memories into luminous auto-biography, the pile of papers lay gathering dust, ignored.

What will happen to them? I asked, what will be their fate in their homeland?

That is anyone's guess, said Yuri Sen, struggling to run a comb through a tiny tangled head.

I will make sure that it is not, said Juan Gorrion.

If they go, he said, I will go with them.

On the day they were to go, I found you and Juan Gorrion, sunk deep in children, entertaining them with unworded gestures, they climbed all over your bodies, poured into the crevices between you, they rhymed and hummed with the music of your lust, I saw you and Juan Gorrion embedded in these doomed children, and I fled.

I returned to London, spent two days locked in the flat, surviving on potato waffles and lemon pickle, lying in the dark, curtains drawn against the obscene peace of the summer evenings, I lay, exhausted of thought, upon my bed, and watched the minutes drip away, and with every minute another thin skin of glass would grow over my pain, so that finally, when

I woke, one morning, to your voices, I felt only a dull calm, the nauseated stillness of a quietened ocean.

You stood in the hallway, your daughter trembling in your arms. Please look after her, you said to me, your eyes wild, for Juan Gorrion had vanished, left without bidding farewell, left only the name of a hotel, and a street, and a town, and a date, under your toothglass. Perplexing, for you had thought he had followed the orphans back to their homeland, but here was an address, at least a thousand miles away, but you would go there, nonetheless, you would cling to this thin trickle of a trail, this meagre spoor, you would follow him into the war-torn lands. Take care of my child, you entreated me, please take care of her.

And what of my autobiography? I asked lamely, selfishly.

Finish it yourself, you said, write it yourself if it means that much to you. You are such a failure, anyway, who will want to read it? Oh, I don't mean that, you said, tears burning your cheeks, you put your arms around my neck and kissed my dazed eyes, take care of her, you whispered hoarsely, and then you were gone.

I have a vision of him waiting, Juan Gorrion, stripped to the waist in a stuffy hotel room, reading Arthur Koestler by the naked overhead light, waiting, waiting. I see him close the book and glance back upon the stretches of his underdocumented life, waiting, waiting. I see him in the bare hotel room, kicking moth corpses under the bed, waiting, waiting. And then suddenly the light shifts, he is drawn to the window, the ivory dusk, Juan Gorrion, seduced by the bloodless sunset, will desert his post, and when you finally enter the room, Juan Gorrion, his eyes packed with lies, will have gone.

We waited, Anya and I, for some word of you, some small sign, and when your daughter first woke to the tartness of green apples in her mouth, she took it to be an omen of your return, for you loved green apples so, had held her high in a Massachusetts orchard many summers ago, your arms dripping apple juice, your cheeks sticky, applebitten, many years ago, she was only eight, you had taken her to pick apples, on one of your few brief visits from England, late in the summer. You had taken her to a friend's farm in Massachusetts, and she had had to leave you a whole day early, for someone was driving to the Jersey coast, she had to leave a day early to save you the journey to Fairhaven, to the house of your parents, where you left her to grow, while you cultivated your own tragedies among the spires of Oxford, taught Russian to lonely, eager faces, and passed the evenings in cidery delight at the Eagle and Child Halls with Sir Percival and his motley satellites.

You never blessed her happiness, you never blessed her pain, on your brief visits she would regale you with small tales, and you would nod and smile and make a mental note of the colour of her knee bruise, kiss her goodnight, and sit to write to Sir Percival: the child has a furious bruise upon her knee, greenblue as diseased violets, that screams her frailty as loudly as her touching attempts to amuse me, to keep me by her side. Once she showed you a poem, her first poem, typed carefully, welted with correction fluid, I will not comment upon it, you told her, taking the paper, I will not tell you how I feel about it, because poetry is a truly personal exercise, and since in your person there must be some kernel of my person, only an utter chaos of emotion can result from my reading your poem, that will undoubtedly obscure its true worth.

Shadows of white oak fractured upon your lips as you told her this: that too much of your own soil was scattered between the sticky sutures of her thoughts. You could not judge her, you could not presume to judge her. And she could not help but feel that it was simply the thinness of your own blood within her poetry that frightened you to such analysis, the horror that your womb might weep such pale tears. She smiled bravely and plucked the sheet from between your fingers, and held it under the kitchen tap, ink dripped onto fresh basil, but Anya's spaghetti sauce did not suffer, no, dinner that evening was heavenly and simple, and as she kissed you goodnight, you said to her, half in penance, half in sorrow, it is time you came with me, it is time I took you away from all this.

My dear, your talents are in working a substance other than language, you told her, something as obdurate as language will only bruise your gentle fingers, it is charcoal and garlic where you are at home, ma petite, sketching and cooking, hopelessly girlish talents, I know, but perhaps you can release them from their feeble reputations . . .

Outside, the New Jersey afternoon began to soften, rising darkness filled the skirtsails of skipping girl children, this skin of peace had papered itself to her imagination, this Anya knew, knew that it would wrap her forever, this barrier of thin calm would lie unblessed between herself and her pain, forever.

And far away in North Oxford, her father sank butter into his parsnips, and wondered, as he did always at Sunday lunch, whether he would ever see her again, whether in his lifetime he would set eyes upon her again, his daughter, child of a strange and fitful union, his daughter, his only uncertainty, gushing sweetly beneath the firm terraces of his existence, his immaculate family, his three sons, all digging into their parsnips, and his wife, chewing slowly beside them, dreaming of violets.

Oh, he had married you and all that, many years ago, when, in a paroxysm of political outrage, the child had been conceived, in a small overheated New Jersey college room. He had married you before the end of his sabbatical, and returned to Oxford, leaving you to finish your research, and nourish the life within you, until she struggled sorely into the world. He did not see her until she was six months old, sprouting pale curls, she surveyed her new world with glossy grey eyes, the wooden cot where she was to learn to sleep while you clicked away beside her on the final draft of your thesis, the fatflowered wallpaper that you would intermittently curse as it flapped over your thoughts. You would grind your cigarette butts into the wheaten carpet, and demand of her, what had you done to deserve this, and she would meet your misery with her large uncomprehending eyes, chuckle dimly and drift back into the intense contemplation of the soothing blankness that was her universe. When she was older, her father would take her into college. She would sit in his rooms and draw, the cookiecutter caps of the stone windows carving the sad skies, he would open large books of maps before her, guide her small hands over the pages, and tell her stories of men who had ventured into the heart of the unknown, simply to seek the source of a river, or to trace the roots of an idea, overgrown with fantasy. It is only a certain peace that I require, he said when he left you, and that peace you will never be able to provide. You sent the child to live with your parents in Fairhaven, New Jersey, and remained, yourself, doggedly in the grim embrace of your new life, which, at twenty-nine, having hurdled marriage and motherhood, seemed only to have begun. For years, you left your daughter with your parents, who loved and ignored her, and spoke in rapid Russian to each other, sealing her into a world of her own small selves, the threads of her being working humbly towards coalition, wrapping slowly into a sibilant whole. For years you left her to the silence of shoreside suburb, and then, finally, last summer you sent her a long-promised one-way ticket to Heathrow, she arrived clutching a large sketchpad, a cloth satchel hanging off a thin shoulder, Yuri Sen had been sent to receive her, with her name written wide on a sheet of paper, she came forward nervously, I am Anya, she said, he rolled the paper into a ball between his palms, and tossed it towards a rubbish bin, he took her hand and raised it to his lips, I am Yuri Sen, he said.

You had been gone for three months when he came. I answered the door expecting Yuri Sen, and was met instead by an anxious pair of eyes, the colour of rubbed slate. I am the goblin under the hill, I thought I heard him say, I am looking for Alexandra Vorobyova.

I had not the courage to turn him away, I told him you were out of town, but invited him in for a cup of tea. I should love a cup of tea, he said, I have just been stuck for an hour on the train from Oxford, there was a bomb in Paddington, it was a nightmare, he said.

Bombs, said Yuri Sen, slotting deftly into the conversation as he came up the stairs with the shopping, bombs have no more effect on the moral condition of the city than bargain bookstores. I am Yuri Sen, he added, setting down his bags, and extended a sore paw.

Robin Underhill, said the stranger, delighted to meet you.

For a year now, I have been recording the insidious growth of bargain bookshops, said Yuri Sen, and believe firmly now that they pose a greater threat to London than the occasional bomb.

The gentleman would like some tea, I said coldly.

You make it, said Yuri Sen, we are in the middle of a discussion, as you can see.

You know very well that I haven't the slightest idea how to make tea, I said.

Oh, very well then, said Yuri Sen, you entertain him, it will be good exercise for your jaws.

It was true that since you had gone, words had shrunken within me into the tight compass of my despair. I had given up going into the laboratory, where all efforts to replicate my results were meeting with utter failure, gold would not become grass, in the presence of any catalyst. No rigid alloy, however carefully constituted, would tip the balance in the favour of synthesis, light would remain light, air would remain air, not an ounce of sugar came of their communion.

You are the famous scientist, are you not? asked Underhill,

uncurling the spine of a monograph on photosynthesis that rested beside him on the couch.

More of a magician than a scientist, I said bitterly.

All the better, he said kindly.

Not when the magic dries up.

What exactly are you trying to do?

Turn sunbeams into treacle, said Yuri Sen, coming in with the tea. For five years now, he has been kept in this chintz dungeon on the promise of turning moonlight into marzipan, and all he has managed to make is molasses out of his life.

You know the old tale of Rumpelstiltskin, said Underhill, swerving politely into fantasy.

There was a miller's daughter, said Underhill, a girl of great beauty. The king, passing by, was naturally captivated, and the miller, in flabbergasted delight, promised that she was able to spin gold out of hay, lest the king doubt that her housewifely skills would match her looks. At this, the king came up with the characteristic fairytale extremes – death if she failed in her task, royal bliss otherwise. I am often exhilarated, said Robin Underhill, by the angularity of these choices, this stern accession to chance – for we are all poised on the brink of disaster, and at the same time on the brink of unimaginable happiness, and yet somehow in this dragonless age, we have learnt to balance, for the most part on that narrow ridge that separates extreme joy from extreme sorrow, to suspend ourselves endlessly at this counterpoint, sighed Robin Underhill.

I saw a shadow swell behind the door, it was Anya, drawn softly to his voice, she stood sucking her thumb, mesmerised.

There she was, then, the miller's beautiful daughter, stuck in a dungeon with a pile of hay to weave into gold. Through one small high window came the afternoon sun, caressing the hay with bright fingers. Only the sun, thought she, can turn anything into gold at its touch, she remembered the wheatfields of her childhood, drenched with golden sunshine, she remembered the flood that had swallowed the fields, brought rot to the crop, it was no wonder that her father had sold her to the king on the absurd promise that she might turn hay into gold, he had eight other children to feed, but I digress, said Robin Underhill.

There was a sound of sobbing, stifled against wood. Underhill leapt up, and looked around, and dashed into the corridor, where he took the weeping girl into his arms, what have they done to you, my darling, he asked, kissing her pale forehead, his hands clenched about the matted mess of her hair, what have they done to you? he roared softly, feeling the ghastly bulge of her small belly, what have you done to her, he asked brokenly, falling onto his knees, who has done this to her? he asked in a small wretched whisper.

You are her father, surmised Yuri Sen grimly.

Of course I am her father, foamed Underhill, who the hell are you?

Anya broke gently away from her father's grasp and moved to stand by him, Yuri Sen. Meekly she took his hand, her eyes swam with fear and fatigue. Cheer up, funnybones, said Yuri Sen, Daddy has come to take care of you.

She buried her face upon his shoulder and began to whimper.

I'm going to take you away, promised her father, still weeping steadily in the dusty hallway, I've come to rescue you from this hell. Your grandparents are frantic, they contacted me in desperation, thank God, where is your damn mother anyway?

She has been spirited away by the puppetmaker, said Yuri Sen gleefully. The Pied Piper has led her away, the man of many dreams, you may remember him from university days, Juan Gorrion.

Not Gorrion, said Underhill, rubbing his eyes, not Juan Gorrion. Of course I remember him, he says softly. He was a great favourite of Partridge's, it's a wonder that they didn't meet before, so she's run off with him, has she?

It's not quite as simple as that, I said defensively.

No, I'm sure it's not, he agreed mournfully. But how could she have left her own child in such a mess?

It's not her fault, for God's sake, she knows nothing about it.

It's not your child, is it? he asked, his chapped lips trembling badly.

No, of course not.

I am the father, said Yuri Sen.

Yes, of course, said Robin Underhill, almost absently. Look, it doesn't really matter whose child it is – you gentlemen will have to let me take her with me. We have a spare room for her, my wife will take care of her, after she's had the baby – which can be given up for adoption – we can think about sending her to college. This is a situation we can rescue, said Robin Underhill. With patience and kindness, we can rescue this situation, I'm sure.

He walked over to where she stood, shivering against the curtains. He took her in his arms and kissed her hair, birds could nest in this, he said, dewing the red mass of curls with easy tears.

You gentlemen won't object, he said, if we leave now.

Not at all, I replied.

Yuri Sen stood silent at the window, his narrow back arched stiffly away from us. Anya took his hand and kissed it, he continued to concentrate on the hoary progress of an old pensioner, labouring towards a pavement mailbox, an airletter gleaming in his faintly oustretched hand.

I read something by Gorrion the other day, said Underhill, it had a clever name – something like 'What Edward said' . . . come, my sweet, we will send for your things later, if that is all right.

We watched them walk down the road, father and daughter, fingers numbly aching in each other's hold. He had not seen her in ten years, not since that furious visit to Fairhaven, one free afternoon during a tedious ethnobotany conference at Columbia.

He had taken the train into the New Jersey suburbs, found the quiet house where she lived with her grandparents, he had only stayed for tea, and she had sat across from him, shyly sucking biscuits, that was the last he had seen of her, ten years ago.

Autobiography, you have consoled me, is a poor means of self-examination, it is only in telling another's story that one can see into oneself. And yet your first novel was about a young Russian emigrée who marries an Englishman and comes to live in London . . . not I, you protest, most certainly not I, why she is a poor forlorn bird, caught between two alien cultures that she had before perceived as one Western entity. She rushes between them, as if between two lovers, or rather two schoolfriends who hate each other, she rushes between them, and is caught in a pendulum motion of petty betrayal, she complains about the lack of mixer taps in Britain, and yet scorns split infinitives, and really she would do well enough without either, for within her the world is still of washtubs and wolves. Certainly she is not I, how else would I have dared to adopt her first person in telling her tale?

Would you have written the story of Robin Underhill's life, if you had spent it with him, if you had not wrenched out your anchor from his small safe world, and cast your sail for emptier islands, that you might populate with your own discordances. Would you have tired of his tale, as you came to tire of mine, or would his past have still enthralled you long after you had grown weary of him, as my past continued to absorb you even after I had begun to pall. The only one of her poems your daughter ever showed you was about an artist, carefully painting a portrait of his lover, every day adding truth to his creation, while the truth of their love fades. You had thought it hackneyed, and been irritated when the image returned, a few months later, as you scrubbed gardenrot from your nails in the cloakroom of Sir Percival's mansion. (*Leave the writing to her, Sir*

Percival had told me that afternoon, leave the writing to Alexandra, who could do a better job on your autobiography than her?) You dried your nails and shook the trembling poem from your head. My daughter finishes school this summer, you told Esha, who was painting her lips beside you, I think it is time she came to live with me.

If I had a daughter, said Esha, I would surely never bear to be apart from her.

Did you try to have children? you asked, or was it simply something you kept putting off?

I had three miscarriages, said Esha, wiping an excess of carmine from her lips.

I'm sorry, you said, taking her free hand, it's just that Anya was so much of an accident – I'm sure if I had had to make the effort, it would never have happened.

You must help me write this book, you said, squeezing her hand. You have shared your life with him, you know him as no one does, you have felt his child growing within you, and that is something, even if you have never carried one to term.

I have felt his children growing within me, said Esha, and I have felt them bleed away, one by one.

It was a month of salt, Esha had said, I would lie in the dark and smile that one and two and four and seven and fourteen made twenty-eight, which any one of them and no other would divide. I would sleep, thinking that if numbers could be so perfect, why not life? And I would pray that each grain of my existence be invested with a limitation rather than an abundance of meaning, perfectly contained within its slight geometry. It was a month of salt, she said, for suddenly the present moment took dimensions, became corpuscular, and seeded with the warmth of destiny.

It was a month of salt, full of small surprises. One morning Esha woke in her mother's arms, her parents had returned a week early from England, where they had gone to settle her brother into his new surrounds – he was to study law from their uncle's home in North London, the crusty old man was pleased to have him, her mother assured her, he had even rented a television so that the boy would not be bored. And her uncle? Esha had wondered, how did he spend his cold evenings in his bachelor home? Reading, endlessly reading, as she would learn later. We used to visit him on Saturdays, in our first few months in London, after lunch he would sit and read, leaving us to our own devices, it was clear he had no use for our company. Esha's brother had disappointed him, marrying a black woman, they had recently emigrated to Canada – at least their mottled brats are more at home in that upstart culture – he spat out when Esha showed him a photograph. We never visited him again. He came to her funeral in a brittle black suit, spoke not a word to me, not a word. He had never respected me anyway, he had always seen through me, known that the real motivation was hers, that I was merely a shell for her purpose, that it was she that had woken one day long ago to the stour stench of paperpulp, and resolved to conquer life, while I was still scraping my knees on gutterboards, looking for precious cricketballs, flicked away into the slime by the neighbourhood nonpareil, to be able to bat even half as well as he, this was the compass of my ambition.

You were telling a story, says Anya, her head upon her father's shoulder, as they wait for the train to Oxford. Will you finish the story of the miller's daughter? pleads Anya, swallowing a cold hunger that creeps up the back of her throat.

The miller's daughter, says Robin Underhill, where did we leave her? Sitting among bright piles of hay, the best, freshest hay that no one in their right minds would think to exchange for gold. She sat and wept into this hay, and her tears released a damp sweetness, that rose and filled the dungeons with the promise of summer. And then she knew, suddenly, that if she spun long enough, she could turn hay into gold. Like a stab of sunlight, it came to her, she would turn hay into gold, it would not be easy, but she would do it.

And so she lifted herself from the hay, sat down at the wheel, took a plump strand, and began to spin. First, it was of no avail, hay remained hay, no matter how fast she spun, she began to wonder if her sudden optimism had not been a manic emotional response to the absurdity of her condition, and then . . . suddenly, the first flecks of gold began to appear, like meek fireflies, and then more, until the strand was bright and heavy in her hands, and bent without breaking into the letters of her name. She worked, and she worked, for three days without pause, till her fingers were raw, and her eyes bleeding from splinters of hay. She spun with a fury that scorched all other emotion, so that when she was finished with the hay, she pulled out in bunches her beautiful red hair, and spun it into copper, a small tangled heap atop the pile of gold. Well, the king was pleased with her after this, but certainly did not want to marry her, for she had turned herself into a bald, bleeding monster. He married a princess from a neighbouring land, which is, I suspect, what he had meant to do anyway.

This is not the story I told you, many years ago, as your bedtime treat, said Underhill, perhaps that is why you are crying, but stories change, my dear Anya, stories change in their telling, and that is why you must never yourself tell the story of your own life, for facts will stretch it taut and motionless, like an empty cloth upon a table, a feast that starves the guest.

Why did you let her go? I asked Yuri Sen.

Who am I to stop her? he answered.

Besides, said Yuri Sen, I am getting a little fed up with all this, to be frank. The way she clings like a thin and treacherous vine, searching the sap of heterosexual passion, when I have only an overwhelming fatherly affection to offer, both to her and our child. I would be quite happy to spend the rest of my life with her, if she did not demand from me the attentions of a lover. I cannot love her, said Yuri Sen.

Sir Percival is going on vacation to Turkey, Yuri Sen continued, he wants me to come with him. I think I should go, it would be rude of me not to.

He picked his long black cape off a dining chair, and draped it over his narrow shoulders. What about you? he asked, what are you going to do?

Now that my past has ceased to be your business, I replied, I see no reason for you to be concerned with my future.

You have till the end of this week, if I am counting right, said Yuri Sen, you have three more days to get your experiments to work. Otherwise, you're toast, my friend, you do realise.

It is not I that was meant to write this, the strange story of my life, not merely because another was charged with the duty of telling this tale, but also because, in truth, I was not meant to live it, I would have cheerfully frittered away my prime stoking a few small comforts: bettering my leg-spin, reading more Tolstoy, picking up a new rhythm on my *tabla*, tinkering in my makeshift laboratory. I was not meant to poach on the territories of creation, not I, I would have buried my nose in the sweet-smelling grass and gone no farther, no serpent could have beguiled me towards knowledge and pain. For me, spring would always have been a carnival of flowers, if I had not, one sticky afternoon, many years ago, walked into my first Chemistry lecture, and fallen in love.

How different it was to this red raw pain that I carry within me now, and call my love for you, this pain that cuts as new glass, how different was what I thought of as my love for Esha, crayoning out like a child's flower from the node of my being, meeting her bright eyes in a delightful confusion of unformed emotion, I placed my books on the bench behind her, and sat riveted by her thick braid swaying like a sluggish snake, as she moved her eyes from blackboard to notebook, and back, taking her first notes. She was only seventeen, it was our first day at college.

She had stood third in the Board examinations, I was told, she was the daughter of the famous barrister, her brother was at Cambridge, whispered my friends in awe, leaving me in a fury of dejection, clinging to the clammy footboard of the route forty-seven bus, I realised I would never dare approach her with my love. My newborn passion, only a few hours old, lay cold, with its wings clipped, in my sweaty palms. At home, they were waiting for stories, three women, my mother, rolling dough for our afternoon savouries, my sister-in-law crouched by the stove, furiously frying, and my sister, still in her high-waisted school uniform, combing out her long shiny hair. He seems a little subdued, my sister-in-law joked, perhaps he has met the girl of his dreams. Indeed I have, I longed to tell them, but how could I ever bring her home to you? Would she not choke upon the kerosene frowst that fills our few rooms, the inscrutable odours that rise from the kidneys of this old house, how would I explain to her that the divan by the dining table was where I slept, where I had been sleeping ever since my brother had married, the previous summer, and moved his monstrous wedding cot into the room that we had shared for so many years, as I would oust my sister from her room, five years later, when Esha and I married, and I brought her to live in these very circumstances that had once sewn so much doubt into my nascent emotions. I hate to displace her, she said of my sister, unwrapping her heavy silks, on the last evening of wedding festivities, her first night in her new home. I took her in my exhausted arms, don't worry about her, I said, she will be married off soon. But I hate to think of her sleeping in the dining room, she needs her privacy, said Esha. Our need is greater, I mumbled, caressing her neck, my hands slipped under her blouse, I felt my passion engulfed by curiosity, we made sweet clumsy love, smiling kindly at each other, and my desire was cocooned in a delicious affection that later came to be its doom.

What became of the miller's daughter? asked Anya.

She spun away, said her father, until her gums sprouted grass from seeds fermenting in the gaps between her teeth, and the king became richer, and richer. He had forgotten all about her, until one bright summer afternoon, when he took a kitchen wench of his fancy down to the dungeons, and burst upon the miller's daughter, still spinning gold from hay, reminding him that the power of all his wealth came from the will of this forgotten creature, sucked dry of her womanhood by the absurd task he had set her, many years ago, when her beauty had blinded him beside the village well where he had stopped to drink on his way back from a hunt.

It is those we love that we long most to punish, said Underhill, you must know this by now, and not always out of perversity, but more I think because it aches to know the limitations and frailties of one held so dear, that she, for whom you might die today, will surely herself one day wither and decay, sprout grass from her gums. It was in rebellion against her morality that the king set the miller's daughter this task, gave her the opportunity to become unreal, which is the preferred state for an object of desire.

(*Tommyrot, says Yuri Sen, and besides what sprite would agree to inhabit the bare corridors of his mind, Robin Underhill, fearful of straying beyond the garden gate of his own dreams.*

Give the man a chance, Yuri Sen!)

I would wake beside your mother, said Robin Underhill, and see worms of dawnlight crawling through her hair, and I would pray that the thick whiteness of her skin might never be soft down for deathmites, the cool circle of her forehead a skating rink for frivolous trematodes, her nailbeds home to woodlice. I would feel the beginnings of you, my dear Anya, stirring within her, and wonder that someday the same womb might be troubled and gnawed by the growing roots of some incurious tree, planted over her grave by those who had loved her. And these were the times when I most felt like breathing poison into her, to still her limbs forever in the frozen delight of sleep, that she might lie ambered within my dreams forever.

Perhaps that is why you left her, said Anya, coughing weakly against her dry fingers.

What, so that I would not have to watch her age and die? Would that it were as trite and simple as that!

Perhaps that is why she left me, said Anya, why you both left me, because you could not bear to watch me grow, write my own poetry, bear my own children.

Forgive me, said Underhill, taking her into his arms, if you can, please forgive me, believe me not a day has gone by that I have not thought of you, my angel, not a single day.

They had just sat down to lunch when he arrived, Yuri Sen, swinging his black cape, he sauntered into the dining room, and seated himself at the far end of the table and ordered Blake to bring him some toast.

This ham is from Catalonia, explained Sir Percival, sliding a silver platter down the length of the table, it gets its special flavour from the snakes the pigs eat, they have specially padded snouts to be able to eat snakes, these Catalan pigs, the ham is delicious, these ladies will not touch it, unfortunately.

The ladies shifted uneasily in their saffron robes at the very thought, there were three of them, one remarkably young for their obviously ascetic profession.

Where are you from, the oldest asked Yuri Sen in cracked Hindi.

Dagenham, replied Yuri Sen, defenceless Dagenham.

The woman frowned and took a large bite out of a slice of melon, not every noun needs a provocative adjective, she said. So her English tutor had told her, many years ago, when she was the young Maharani of N——, the delicious precocious wife of the King Kortobbo Bemurah, how he had adored her, pandered to her ravenous appetite for accomplishment, filled the palace with language and music tutors, brought in embroiderers and carvers, that she might be schooled in every possible art. And yet she had relinquished all, to bear the king his four sons, all of whom had betrayed her, joined the Leftist political party that had briefly imprisoned her, years ago. Years ago, all of it, most of her life, was years ago, years ago, years ago she had discovered the divine child, the young woman who sat at her side, nibbling on melon, found her in a dusty village, discoursing on the *Bhagavadgita* with the village elders, she was only five. The dowager took her home, the grimy child, upturned nose clotted with green snot, paid her miserable parents a thousand rupees, and dragged her into the white Ambassador, she can recite all of the *Ramayana* and the *Mahabharata*, her father promised, trembling with excitement. The queen mother took the child back to her sandstone castle, locked her in a room of marble, with paper and ink, and a golden fountain pen, and told her that if she did not have the entire *Ramayana* written out by the morrow, she would be donated to a beggar-lord, maimed and sent to beg in the streets. But I cannot write, the poor child protested. At this, the dowager summoned her servants and bade them provide her with a tape-recorder and an endless spool of tape. And indeed, in the morning, they found her asleep, by the recorder, exhausted from regurgitating the entire epic onto magnetic tape. The dowager could barely contain her excitement, but exercised restraint, and delivered her next challenge: to recite the entire *Mahabharata*, which of course would take more than one night. Three nights she was given, upon meagre rations, lest the splendour of palace food distract her, three nights, and when she emerged, she could barely stand upon her small legs, collapsed against the balcony rails, where she was plied with soft drinks and sweetmeats, while the dowager fastforwarded through the *Mahabharata*, and came, long before the tapes ended, to prostrate herself at the child's feet. But the little girl barely noticed, for her attention, renewed by glucose, had been siphoned towards the garden where the dowager's grand-daughter was bathing her Smurf.

What a lovely toy! she exclaimed.

You shall have as many Smurfs as you want, the dowager promised, a family, nay, an army of Smurfs, promised the widow of King Kortobbo Bemurah.

Not a day has passed, said Robin Underhill to his daughter, that I have not thought of you, of your chubby childcheek cradled in my hand, a porcelain dream.

We are here, he continued, back in the city of spires where you passed your infancy, perhaps you have not been back since?

Was that why you left her? asked Anya, because she was deviating so consummately from your image of her, is that why you left my mother?

No, said Robin Underhill, I left her because she broke things and smashed plates, I cannot stand the noise of breaking glass. For a long time I waited for her to leave me, I was sure she would, but then I could bear it no longer, I left her, my dear, because she could see no path through the trees but her own.

They have been Smurf-shopping in New York, explained Sir Percival to Yuri Sen, of his unlikely guests.

Do you often retreat to that concrete jungle? asked Yuri Sen, politely, reaching for the spinach pancakes.

The young woman, matron saint of Kortobbo Bemurah, stood up and shook her long flowing hair loose. He is the devil, she declared in Hindi, *shaitan* himself.

She says he is the devil, explained the dowager to her host.

Yes of course, said Sir Percival jovially.

The girl began to drum on the table with her fork, he is the devil, she repeated darkly, it is he who has besmirched the purity of our land with wave upon wave of filthy invaders, he has brought the dark age, *kali yuga*, upon us, he has sucked dry the blood of our oxen, and filled their veins with rosewater, he has buttered the winds with evil, that shakes out strange melodies from our very own musical instruments . . .

Shut up, you silly cow, said Yuri Sen.

The woman began to foam at the mouth, shaking her thick mass of jet hair.

You'd better leave, said Sir Percival to Yuri Sen.

This is it, said Robin Underhill, pulling into the driveway, we moved here about five years ago, the basement is almost a flat unto itself, my mother-in-law used to live in it in perfect isolation, she died last year quite suddenly, we still haven't cleared her things out, but you can do it up as you like, there's no central heating I'm afraid, we keep meaning to extend the system into the basement, just haven't got round to it yet – I must tell you it was hard on the conscience, sitting warm and cosy upstairs, with the old woman, my mother-in-law I mean, huddling by the gas fire in her rooms below, I hope you won't be cold my dear, perhaps we'll sort out the central heating finally, now that you're here.

He led her into the kitchen, through the hallway, poured two glasses of orange juice, handed her the taller of them. Are you hungry? he asked.

The sound of gravel crunching under car wheels made him twitch suddenly, he took her hand and led her quickly out into the hallway and down the stairs into the basement, sat her down upon a narrow bed, she felt herself sinking into egg-pudding softness. Stay here, her father told her, rest, it's better if I first explain about you to my wife.

You had better leave, said Sir Percival to Yuri Sen, his eyes the same ice that they had been, seven years ago, when he had banished from this very table, Yuri's weeping fiancée, fair Fiona, blubbering into her cornflakes, still half within the clutches of drugged sleep, for you, Alexandra Vorobyova had the previous evening crushed codeine into her cocktails at Sir Percival's request, get her away from him, he had whispered, get that chirpy idiot away from him. In earthwounded Birbhum, he had loved her, Yuri Sen, pledged eternal love among small frozen earthquakes, the pale Fiona, drawn by some terrible translations of Tagore to the redsoil of the poet's dreams, she had come to spend a few months in Shantiniketan, and there met him, Yuri Sen, in his final year of his Statistics degree. They had returned to England together, engaged. And so they had remained, in joyous inbranching innocence, until that Sunday morning when she drove away alone, blindly weeping, from Sir Percival's estate where he would remain, Yuri Sen, for seven long years, above an aviary, upon floors of glass. Get her away from him, Sir Percival had urged you, what is doing with *her*? And you had taken pestle to mortar, spiked her Sidecar with codeine, sent her reeling into hard black dreamlessness, from which she woke with cracked porcelain eyes, head heavy, wits chuzzled, and her lover, overnight, the stranger that he was always meant to be. You had better leave, Sir Percival had told her, when she began to weep into her cereal at breakfast, she had gazed imploringly at Yuri Sen, calmly chewing on black pudding, he had looked back, his eyes clear and bright, finally unburdened of cosmic ideals, you take the car, he had suggested, I can catch the train later.

So you're not coming with me? said Fiona.

No, said Yuri Sen.

The smell of cheap wax is dense upon the pillows, Anya feels the orange juice bubbling thickly inside her, upstairs her father is talking to his wife, she cannot hear what he says, but his voice darts and quivers around the nylon patchwork of the tense bedspread, she knows he cannot tell his wife who is in their basement, a heart within a heart, throbbing madly under the floorboards, can he hear her retch? Does he tremble at the sound of puddling vomit? She knows he cannot confess to his wife that his past lies speckled with its future in their basement, Eleanor, he begins . . . but she speaks in a rapid uninterruptible stream about departmental tensions, the rising volume of traffic, the ill health of the Vice Chancellor's dog. When she stops to breathe, Eleanor Underhill, her thoughts are crowded by the sanctity of violets, can you microwave parsnips, d'you think? she asks him, and her laughter is like a finger of old moonlight poking a rusty can.

Before he leaves, Yuri Sen is handed a letter by the butler, Blake, in it a butterfly-shaped card, an invitation to his sister's wedding, Luna Sen, to be joined in holy Brahminic union, with Partha Barua, young pimply Pat, had they fallen in love? an engineered romance? Pat Barua! How could she? The wedding is this evening, he notes, he feels a strange urge to show up at the North London Hall, he watches with puzzle-ment a strange desire grow within him to see her, his sister, Luna, he has not spoken to her in seven years. He remembers their childhood, among carpets smelling of fried cardamom, playing endless board games, and scorning each other's friends. She was always closer to Sputnik, he would surely have come over from the States for her wedding, Sputnik Sen, in his Stanford sweatshirt, no that was seven years ago, he had last seen him, in his green sweatshirt, home for the summer, he was clipping the hedge when they left, Fiona blew him a kiss, we'll probably be back late, she said. What's the guy's name again, asked Sputnik, whose house you're going to, something funny, like Ostrich or something? Partridge, she replied, Percival Partridge, his parties are reputed to be out of this world . . .

The front door bangs, the house is still again, his wife has gone to pick the children up from school. Robin Underhill descends, mirthlessly into the basement, where she is sitting, on the cold floor, her head upon the bedside table, cheek clammy against formica, his daughter, Anya. He takes her hand, crouching beside her, are you all right? he asks.

I want to go back to London, she says firmly.

He stands up and walks towards the squat window, eye-level with the back lawn, he leans his forehead upon his hands against the cold ledge, he sighs, I could give you about five hundred pounds, he says, would that see you through for a month or so, I can give you more later, but hopefully your mother will be back soon, what you should do is have the baby here and then go back to the States and forget all about this, go to college, start a new life, leave all of this behind, none of this is your fault, Anya, none of it.

I'd like to go back to London, says Anya, through clenched teeth.

Well, come on then, says her father, let's get out of here before they get back.

He leads her to the kitchen, and cuts her a slice of thick fruitcake, you must be starving, he says, eat this quickly, while I get the money.

She raises a fat morsel to her lips, swallows grimly, her father reappears with an envelope – here you are, five hundred pounds, and this is my phone number at work. If you're ever in trouble, just phone me, and see if you can get the phone in that flat reconnected, I could call you, then, every day.

We'd better go, he says, I can wrap the cake up for you, if you like, there's some fruit here as well, if that's what you'd prefer. Tell you what, I'll just pop a few things into this for you, he shakes out a Marks & Spencer's plastic bag, and fills it with fruit and odds and ends from the refrigerator – there, that should keep you going for a bit, he says, placing the bag gently between her ice-cold fingers.

He remembers an incident from their childhood, on holiday in Calcutta, Luna had trapped a befuddled bird under a bamboo wastebasket, their grandfather took Luna and Sputnik to Lake

Market to buy it a cage, and meanwhile he, young Yuri Sen, released the creature from its pretty prison, coaxed it to fly away, for it was still in a state of avian shock, its senses tightened into its gizzard. You must have let it go! screamed Luna, when they returned with their empty cage, you must have released it!

Birds should be free, said Yuri Sen.

I was getting ready to boil an egg when he returned, Yuri Sen, put in a couple for me, he said, unwrapping his black cape. I didn't get any lunch, some saffron-clad loonies convinced Sir Percy that I was the devil.

A minor bit of brainwashing compared to what their brothers have achieved at home, I said. They have demolished the mosque, I told him, throwing him the newspaper. His face darkened as he read, I don't believe this, said Yuri Sen.

It is a joke, he said, it is almost a joke when a bunch of fanatics claim that a mosque is occupying the birthsite of their mythic hero, you are almost thankful for these remnant flecks of the surreal, at least at the dinner table, when your heart is pounding and your mouth is dry, you are thankful for these absurdities, hooray for hysteria, and then, before you know it, the margins have closed, the country is in spasm, the cardboard horse has stepped down from the stage and is violently raping your wife, the chamberpiece has become a symphony, the chamberpot is the nation's fingerbowl, and we hang our heads in stupid shame.

We have to be out of here by midnight, I told him, Chearsley just came by.

Where will you go? he asked.

To Esha's uncle, I replied, I have phoned him. I should be able to get a flight back to Calcutta next week.

At least we do not have to worry about the girl, said Yuri Sen.

The doorbell rang, Yuri went to answer it, I started to peel the eggs. My God, it's you, I heard him say, for one brief

moment my heart leapt at visions of you, travelweary, at the
door. It's Anya, said Yuri Sen, coming back with a plastic
bagful of odd bits of food, it's Anya, she's come back.

He extracted a halfeaten jar of lumpfish caviare from the
jumbled goodies. What will we do with her? asked Yuri Sen.

She drifted in like a small pale stalk, noded clumsily at the
waist, came into my arms, and crying softly, said, I will never
leave again, I promise. She began to shake badly, her cry rose to
a thin wail, sheeted in pain, I will die if you leave me, she said.
Yuri Sen, suddenly overcome, licked the fishspawn off his
finger, and came and took us both in his jointed embrace, His
arms encircled us like the jaws of some fragile prehistoric beast
held wide to the public, he laid his long cheek against Anya's
hair, we will all go to Calcutta, he declared, it is our only hope.

Over egg sandwiches, she told us her father had given her
five hundred pounds. She produced the envelope from her jacket
pocket, five hundred pounds, we're getting somewhere, said
Yuri Sen, I'm sure I can ask Sir Percy for the rest of our fares.

I had two thousand pounds in my bank account, but was not
inclined to tell him. Somewhere I nourished the small hope that
I would return to London, if only to find you, and God knows I
would need it then.

(*You bastard, says Yuri Sen, I could have been saved all that trouble,
you creepy bastard.*

*Then there might not have been a story, if it had all been so simple,
think of it this way, Yuri Sen.*

*There would have always been a story, he replies, even if we had spent
our lives drinking tea around an octagonal table, there would still have
been a story.*

*Remember this, says Yuri Sen, before you there was your story, your
story always takes first place.*)

I'm sure I can get the money from old Perce, said Yuri Sen.

Chearsley had appeared, that afternoon, as the clock was
chiming four, nervously pinstriped, eternal messenger, he had

produced the papers from his briefcase without many prelimi-
naries, come to kick you out, I'm afraid, he said, mildly
apologetic. Funny, isn't it, he says, seems only yesterday that I
chased you down in Calcutta, got you all organised to come
here. Shame about the experiments, everyone was so excited
about them, then, even I, I mean I didn't understand any of it,
but there was a strange hope in it, for all of us, because scientific
discoveries nowadays, I mean, they aren't like they used to be,
like someone finding a vaccine against smallpox, or a cure for
syphilis. All my life I expected to witness something of that
magnitude, if you know what I mean, and with you, I thought
we were on the brink of something like that, you know, the end
of an era, an age of new hope, a brave new world, and to think it
had all worked in your garage in Calcutta, lamented Chearsley.

We shook hands at the door. Better luck next time, said
Chearsley.

He does not want to speak to you, said Blake of his master. Yuri
Sen squirmed and swore within the cramped phonebooth, tell
him it's urgent, he commanded Blake.

He says everything is urgent with you, Blake reported after a
few minutes.

Damn him, I'm running out of change, tell him . . . oh, look
I'll ring you back, just try and convince him to take the call next
time.

I shall do nothing of the sort, said Blake, I am his butler, not
his private secretary.

Damn you, said Yuri Sen.

Where to, then, but North London, where his sister,
bejewelled, awaits their childhood friend, Partha Barua,
panhandling Pat, still struggling with unfamiliar folds of white,
in the bedroom of his uncle's flat, his seven sisters giggling shyly
in the hallway, Pat Barua is fearfully late for his wedding, soon
the holy hour will have passed, leaving his bride, Luna Sen,

stale, blinking behind her new contact lenses. Where is he? they ask, the bewildered hordes, will you all please leave me alone, pleads Luna Sen, please I want to be alone.

She sits in the corner of the dusty Green Room of the Community Hall, eyes thick in the gold of her arm, turns sharply at the sound of footsteps. Yuri! she exclaims, Yuri, she pleads, get me out of here, please!

Swiftly, he reaches behind to turn the key in the lock, and then stares thoughtfully at the window, I remember climbing out through there, he tells her, his sister Luna Sen, his first words to her in seven years.

That was a summer, many years ago, a summer of dense expectation. He had just taken his A-levels, had an offer from Cambridge, and had been called upon by his parents' friends to play the undemanding role of a Buddhist sage in the Tagore dance drama they were to perform on the fortieth anniversary of the poet's death. In this very Community Hall, they had rehearsed, Tuesdays and Thursdays, within these musty walls he had developed a deep obsession for the young wife of a Bengali accountant, the terribly talented Madhuri Sen (that she should share his surname was a horrible irony), who played mother to the untouchable Chandalika, the young girl who brings water to the thirsty sage, drythroated young Yuri, dying of desire for Madhuri Sen. He wondered, picking his way through the baffled wedding guests, whether she was among them, Madhuri Sen, once splendid in sorcery, waving her dark limbs in the ecstasy of madness, using all her powers to convoke the Buddhist wanderer who had veined her daughter's heart in iron, the tired pilgrim, Yuri Sen. He had A's in Physics, Maths and Chemistry, I would like to go to Shantiniketan, he told his proud parents, I want to learn to be a Bengali, said Yuri Sen. What of Cambridge? they had asked in desperation. Cambridge is boring, declared Yuri Sen. He would go to Shantiniketan, where Madhuri had spent her childhood and her universities, return worthy of her, and much else, but mainly her, though fate had already snatched her away from the compass of his future. Where is she now, Madhuri, if not among the patient guests? Buffalo, New York, is the answer, but this Yuri Sen does not know. Madhuri Sen, he still sees, in the colours of flaming earth, gathering her magic into a dark noose to pull about her daughter's distant beloved, the Buddhist pilgrim, played with feverish calm by young Yuri Sen. He would come whirling in from the stage wings to fall at her exhausted feet, Madhuri Sen, driven to sin by her daughter's desire, the unfettered passion of an untouchable maiden. And what had he done to unleash such a torrent of longing? Simply asked for a drink of water, the Buddhist monk, played by Yuri Sen, had confronted the young untouchable girl as she was bathing their orphan calf, bestowed upon her the privilege of quenching a human thirst, always denied to her unclean caste. Can the darkness of cloud besmirch rain? she asks her mother, crazed by her new dignity, crippled by desire for he who, by consenting to drink from her impure hands, had raised her to the status of a human, *the flower says I am eternally beholden to earth, but let me forget that I have been conceived in dirt, for I am pure . . .* what is this language you speak? her mother asks, terrified. I no longer understand you, I no longer know you. And behind black curtains young Yuri Sen stifled dry and strange sobs that rose to this throat at this verdict, Yuri Sen, his unripe Bengali acid upon his tongue, struggling with the tentacles of an unslept dream in the dusty Green Room of a North London Community Hall. Where else might he have found himself on this day, of all days, the day of his eviction from his erstwhile Eden, the green infolding expanse of Percival Partridge's kingdom, where else might he find himself but between the very walls that flanked his first search for identity, where he had once stood, his cosmic ideals unspent, and craved the butterbroth of a tropical past.

He lifts the sash window, and peers out into the April evening, we can get out this way, he assures his sister. She looks around, eyes the open window sceptically, but then stands up and totters heavily under her silks and jewels towards him, as silently as her trinkets will allow, swivels with surprising ease upon the sill, and is standing in the urine stench of the back alley before he has time to consolidate his plan of escape. He climbs out beside her, takes her bracelet-choked arm, and leads her around a stark corner, and through a rusty gate into the beer garden of the Dog and Dumpling.

The keenest moments of his youth lay buried in time within this unholy space, that afternoon when the music director had turned up with a synthesiser, and Madhuri Sen had erupted in a blaze of indignation, stalked out of the rehearsal, Yuri Sen following, trembling with excitement. Let's have a drink, he had suggested, and she, feeling passionately liberated, had agreed to air her grievances within the smoky confines of the Dog and Dumpling. What will you have? he had asked tenderly, a beer, she had replied recklessly, and Yuri Sen, realising the limitation of her acquaintance with alcohol, had wickedly brought her a pint of Tennent's Extra, which had released from within her a homesickness so strong that Yuri Sen had almost gagged upon the weight of her emotion. How will I ever make my home here? she had asked him, how will I ever communicate with these ignorant, insensitive beasts, who treat Tagore as if he were public property? Is he not, Yuri Sen had wondered, is he not everyman's poet, Rabindranath Tagore? A synthesiser, Madhuri Sen had fumed, is nothing sacred? She had withdrawn from the dance drama, as had Yuri Sen, many years ago. They had shaken hands over their decision in the Dog and Dumpling, at the corner table where now a bandaged punk lurks like some damaged relic in a miser's cottage. Yuri Sen pulls out a plush stool for his sister, whose absurd garb attracts many baleful but brief stares, she sits down heavily with her back to them all, what will you have to drink? he asks.

Gin and tonic, she says, and some crisps please, I haven't eaten since daybreak.

He flings her a few packs from the counter as he waits for

the drinks. She has gone through two of them by the time he returns, I loathe cheese and onion, she says, cramming her mouth with crisps, trust you to forget.

It's been seven years, he says, you might have developed quite a taste for them in this time. You look the same, he adds, somewhat absently.

Even in this get-up? asks Luna Sen.

He lights a cigarette, why are you marrying Pat? he asks.

Because I trust him, she says.

With what? he asks.

I feel I know him, she continues, I have never felt like I've known anybody that well in my life.

Fiona thought she knew me, says Yuri Sen, and she was wrong.

I thought I knew you, says Luna Sen.

You probably did, better than most. I was the bastard who let your bird go, I was the tormented soul who scoffed at your emotional excesses, I was the circle of reason that became a noose.

Fiona is at the wedding, she says.

I did not notice her.

I am sure she noticed you.

What is she doing with herself these days?

Do you care?

No, says Yuri Sen, sadly. Can I get you another drink?

Yes please, and more crisps.

He returns this time with salt and vinegar, I could eat a horse, she says, her bangles clanking as she rips the packets open.

And what about you, are you still with the same woman? his sister asks.

What woman?

Whoever you left Fiona for, she replies, through a mouthful of mush.

I did not leave Fiona for anyone, says Yuri Sen.

But there is another woman in your life, insists his sister.

There is a girl, he answers, looking into his beer. She is seventeen, she's pregnant.

You should marry her, she says grimly.

I don't love her, he says.

I see.

He lights another cigarette. I need money, Luna, he says, Sir Percival has kicked me out.

Well, can't you get a job?

With a degree in Statistics from Shantiniketan? In this market?

You will have to get a job, she says. She traces one of the many lines of gold around her neck, finds the clasp and pulls it to the front, unhooks it, and hands him a heavy emerald-studded necklace, the only piece of jewellery that their grandmother never pawned. Have this, she says, her eyes gleaming with a manic tenderness.

He fingers the necklace, the frail emeralds and disdainful pearls, clenched within heavy gold. Many years ago it had graced his grandmother's young pale neck, on the day of her wedding, this monstrous piece of jewellery that she would later come close to pawning to buy her son a dissection kit. Her hands had brushed against its lethal coils, and withdrawn in despair. I have nothing, she had declared to her fatherless child, and Dr Sen, later of Dagenham, had struggled through Intermediate Biology on borrowed scalpels, all so that his mother could present his bride with this necklace of pearl and emerald, this aged ornament that cowers now between Yuri Sen's long fingers. He spreads it out upon his thigh, it has majesty, decides Yuri Sen.

Look who's here, says Luna Sen, he could always smell us out, couldn't he, even when he was a child, and we were trying desperately to get rid of him, he would always find us, she says of Sputnik Sen, staggering towards them in his Brooks Brothers suit. How the hell did know we'd be here? she asks him.

Pat's here, says Sputnik, collapsing onto a stool.

Like a drink? asks Yuri Sen, drawing his cape over his jewelled thigh.

Surely it's too late, says Luna Sen, surely the appointed, anointed hour has passed, the Brahmin has packed his bags and gone home . . .

The Brahmin has found some way of getting around the time problem, splutters Sputnik Sen, through several sips of Yuri's beer, it has something to do with the complex rotation of the planets, man, what a kook, laughs Sputnik Sen.

And suddenly, for an imprecise moment, they are a united family, sharing a rational joke, a frame in the reel is replaced by an old snapshot, just one frame, lurching inexorably towards the next, where, once again, the seven years of his prodigality will sit between them like a bladder of raw blood, once more, he is unforgiven, Yuri Sen.

She stands up and shakes her silks. Well, I'd better go and get married then, she says.

She begins to walk towards the door, Sputnik drains Yuri's glass, are you coming back with us? he asks.

Yuri Sen shakes his head.

He sits for a while after they have gone, staring proverbially into his empty glass, until it is whisked away by a surly barmaid in ginger leggings, who wipes the table down with vigour, knocking a soggy cardboard beermat onto his lap. He picks it up and twirls it between his fingers, to his horror its underside advertises a local bargain bookshop, 'literally a bargain' it proclaims in ciderbled blue, he takes it in his hands and crushes it into a small ball, tosses it into an abandoned wineglass, and leaves the Dog and Dumpling with tears in his eyes and his grandmother's jewels in his pocket.

We had our bags packed by the time he returned, I had phoned Esha's uncle to ask if I could bring with me the daughter of a friend, left in my care. She is unwell, I had explained. There was no question of asking him to offer shelter to Yuri Sen, where will you go? I asked him, as he loaded our bags into the minicab, I have friends, he answered mysteriously. We left him standing grimly on the kerbside, his black cape flying in the dark wind. Will I ever see him again? asked Anya, tears flowing down her thin cheeks, will I ever see him again?

Esha's uncle greeted me grimly, offered us cold lentils for supper, I myself only take a glass of milk in the evenings, he told us. Anya was too exhausted to eat, he took her up to her room, there is some hot water if you want a bath, he suggested kindly, although you look as if you might fall asleep in the tub.

Who is she? he asked me, she has the face of an angel.

Her mother is a writer, I said, she has been missing for a few months.

What will you do with her? he asked.

Take her with me, I suppose. I promised her mother I would look after her.

I poured salt over my lentils, is there any butter? I asked.

Promothesh, he said suddenly, Promothesh, they demolished the *masjid*.

Yes, I know.

They destroyed it with their bare hands, he said slowly, tracing the cherubs on the wallpaper with his walking stick.

I lifted a forkful of rice and lentils to my lips, do you have any butter or mustard oil? I asked.

I was passing by some cheap television shop on the High Street when I saw them, said Esha's uncle, there on the ghastly screen, the frenzied crowds attacking the *masjid*. I came home as fast as my creaky legs would allow, and sat in a daze, there in that armchair, my head felt hollow, my heart was thumping, and I felt – as I have never done before – eager for more news, eager to witness this carnage, eager to *see* what my heart and head refused to believe. Can you believe this, Promothesh, I even went as far as to drag out from the boxroom the defunct television set that your father-in-law had purchased so many years ago for his hapless son, hoping for some small flicker, some porridge of black and white dots that would somehow take me closer to the scene of the tragedy. Of course the dreadful thing did not even turn on, although it had been in perfect order when I had consigned it to the boxroom, fifteen years ago when the boy ran off with the negress. I had always despised television, tolerated it only for the sake of that ingrate, but here I was today trying desperately to breathe some life into its horrible carcass, just in case it might still work, in the hope that it might compress my distress into some blurry image, that horror made palpable might be easier to bear than horror in the abstract. Of course I gave up soon enough, I was sitting with my head in my dusty and bruised hands when you telephoned, said Esha's uncle.

I raked together the last of my lentils and swallowed them in one brave gulp.

You caught me in a very vulnerable state, said Esha's uncle. Otherwise I am not sure I would have entertained such an unusual request.

We were unexpectedly evicted, I told him stiffly, I could not think of where else to go.

I am glad of your company tonight, Promothesh, the old man replied, I am glad of the angelic young girl sleeping upstairs. On this dark day you appear to me like beacons of hope, but any other time I might have told you to go away and leave me alone, a dry brain in a dry season, this has always been my fate, but the winds have turned Promothesh, nothing will be any more as it always has been.

For a week we heard nothing from him, Yuri Sen, we had given up hope, when suddenly the doorbell rang, and there he was, in his long black cape, with the air of a vagabond returned rich from his travels, he handed the taxi driver an extravagant tip and stepped inside sniffing disdainfully, after carefully wiping his new Ralph Lauren shoes on the ailing doormat. He peeled off his new silklined calf-leather gloves, and showed me his bruised palms, some vandals tried to crucify me, he said, the night that we parted. I met with a pack of demented skinheads, they pushed me up against a wall, and threatened to crucify me, but thankfully they only had drawing pins.

An opportune burst of police sirens had sent them flying, and Yuri Sen, his grandmother's necklace throbbing in his pocket, had climbed up the nearest fire escape, and finding a half-open window, had jumped in through it into the offices of the United Leaseholders and Realtors Organisation, where he had spent a restless night in fear that the skinheads would any moment resume their pursuit of him. They had seen him scaling the fire escape, knew full well he was trapped inside this building, but something kept them back from smashing in one of the windows, and impaling him upon the plush carpet in the chambers of the United Leaseholders and Realtors Organisation, something protected him here, he did not know what. He crouched underneath one of the desks, and allowed himself to be lulled to sleep by the blasts of heat from a nearby duct. He was woken by the roar of a vacuum cleaner, the cleaning woman gasped as the nozzle hit his knees, please do not be afraid, said Yuri Sen.

He explained his strange predicament to her, that he had been on his way home when he had been attacked by a pack of hooligans. This was my only route of escape, he told her, I can't even be sure they aren't waiting for me outside. Look at what they did to me, said Yuri Sen, holding out his hands, caked in dried blood. Later, drinking tea in her flat, his hands bathed and bandaged, he had confessed to her that he had not been on his way home at all, but wandering aimlessly, having been evicted that very afternoon from his overmortgaged home. He was the last in a long line of feudal lords, he told her, and all he had left now was this last jewel, he had said to her, pulling out his grandmother's necklace from his pocket. She gasped as he laid it out upon the formica countertop, is it real? she asked.

Real! he snorted, it is more real than either you or I.

What are the green stones, she asked.

Emeralds, he said gently.

How old is it? she asked.

I believe it was crafted on the occasion of my grandmother's wedding, that would be a good sixty years ago, she was fifteen at the time, and astonishingly beautiful, exceptionally pale in complexion with unusual green eyes. My grandfather saw her at the theatre in Calcutta and declared he would marry no other, even though she came from rather an undistinguished background, while my grandfather, as I have mentioned, was no less than a feudal prince. He loved her madly, insisted that she continue to be privately educated while she bore him six sons. He employed tutors for English, French, piano, and even Mathematics, all of which came in very handy after he died, when Bengal was partitioned and the family completely dispossessed. She gave private tuition and sold all her jewels to put her sons through college, all except this, for this was her father's gift to her, who had spent the rest of his life at the mercy of the moneylenders just so that he might present his favourite daughter with emeralds to match the unusual green of her eyes.

Your eyes have some green in them, she said.

You can see it better in direct sunlight, said Yuri Sen. But yes, I resemble her rather strongly, they say, my green-eyed grandmother, this jewel cost her father so dearly that he was never able to marry off his two other daughters, they became schoolteachers, helped bring up my father and his brothers when they were orphaned, spinster aunts to the rescue. Of course their nephews never took care of them when they were old, they lived upon their meagre pensions in a dingy little flat near their old school. We would go and visit them on our holidays in India with some terrible gift, a pair of cheap cardigans or a set of plastic picnic mugs, drink the salty tea they offered us, and make desperate conversation. They both sang beautifully but I only found this out after they were dead, when my brother Sputnik took it into his head to rescue some old spool tapes that my father had stashed away in the attic, he borrowed an ancient tape player off his drama teacher and arranged our cassette player so that we could rerecord the contents of the spool tapes, and amid the motley fragments of family conversations, stuttery recitations, play readings, we discovered songs that our great-aunts had sung with profound grace, Tagore songs of great passion that moved me, in particular, to tears, for I had just returned from three years at the poet's university, and nothing could have brought back the smells of Shantiniketan more keenly to me than the un-expectedly beautiful voices of my great-aunts raised in unison to celebrate the mysteries of the universe as the poet would have, *you clothed him as a beggar in your game, the skies reeled with laughter, you filled his beggar's bowl with scraps, only so that you might steal his alms.* We crowded around the tape recorders, and I felt myself transported back to a time in my life that never had been, could see that my brother and sister too were in some small way sucked into this space of unrealised memory, while the woman I was to marry that summer, pale Fiona, hovered politely somewhere beyond the edges of this vortex. This is not a bad thing, I had reasoned to myself, why should I expect to share everything quite so intensely with her, why indeed, was it not precisely that interval of incomprehension that would forever feed our passion? The tape reached its end, my brother Sputnik switched off the machines, and headed off to trim the hedges, my sister Luna declared that she was going to take an afternoon nap, I looked at my watch and suggested to Fiona that we get going, we had been invited to a party in the country, it would be nice to beat the traffic, I told her. She left to dress, and I turned on the old tape player and wound the tape back to listen again to the lost voices of my father's maiden aunts, *the skies reverberated with laughter, you let him fill his beggar's bowl with scraps, only so that you might steal his alms,* Fiona reappeared in an avocado-coloured summer dress, a wide lilac hat in her hands, we stepped out into the emollient sunlight, Sputnik clipping the front hedge in his green Stanford sweatshirt, home from college for the summer, Fiona blew him a kiss, we'll probably be back late, she said. What's the guy's name again, asked Sputnik, whose house you're going to, something funny, like Ostrich or something? Patridge, Fiona replied, Percival Partridge, his parties are reputed to be out of this world . . .

Your country seems to be up in flames, his benefactress said to Yuri Sen, distracted from his narrative by Breakfast TV, your country looks to be in a mess, she said chewing on a piece of toast.

I must go back, he told her, I need to go back, my people are dying, killing each other, a great shadow has fallen over my land.

She looked at him with sorrow, how will you go back if you have no money? she asked.

I must sell the necklace, said Yuri Sen.

She gasped, I see, she said.

Can you help me? he asked, do you know anyone who deals in such things?

What do you mean, she asked, why can't you just sell it to a jeweller if you want to.

To sell something like this legitimately is no simple matter, said Yuri Sen, I will need all sorts of documents that I simply do not have.

I see, she said. I suppose I could phone my brother, she said after a while.

I knew you would be able to help me, said Yuri Sen, the moment the nozzle of your vacuum cleaner brushed against my leg and I looked up into your face, I knew you would save me.

She got up without a word and left the room to phone her brother, Yuri Sen found himself alone with the television,

Calcutta was under curfew, the camera meandered aimlessly through the silent city, nothing looks familiar, thought Yuri Sen.

She returned with cups of fresh coffee, my brother will meet you here at noon, she told him.

They drank the coffee in silence. Then she asked, all this stuff about your grandmother, it's all rubbish isn't it?

Every word I have said is true, declared Yuri Sen.

It took a few days to sell the necklace, and all this time Yuri Sen never left her flat, he slept on the couch and watched television all day, watching the crisis deepen in his country, and then falter and quieten. How can all of this really end? he would wonder, will we finally endure the ultimate fall, or will some strange force of our histories weave us back into a chaotic whole, will we ever rise again or will we now dissolve slowly into the ashes of our past, he would wonder. And at times he felt a strange longing for Anya, for the quiet circle of her thin arms around her knees to bury his thoughts within, the clumsy bulge of her pale belly swelling with his child, he craved the ghostly emanations of her virginal grief, his life was now bound to hers through threads of unlikely glass, he decided, their alliance was as arbitrary and magical as that of a word and its meaning, thought Yuri Sen.

With the money he first bought a pair of gloves, for the ones he owned had been rudely punctured by the skinheads, calf-leather gloves lined with cool silk to soothe his sore palms. He then purchased a black silk turtleneck shirt and a pair of black trousers, some new socks and a pair of extremely expensive shoes. He bought a leather bag in which to stuff his old clothes, and caught a cab to North London, and arrived at our door, where is she? he asked, stepping into the dark hallway. Anya appeared like a cloudy apparition at the head of the stairs, let's go for a walk, he said to her. Without hesitation she grabbed her coat, and walked out upon his arm into the miserable afternoon. Who is he? asked Esha's uncle, after the door had shut behind them, who is he, he smells like the devil, said Esha's uncle, he smells like old leather made new.

You dressed him as a beggar in your great game
The skies convulsed with laughter
Many roads has he travelled, knocking on many doors
Filling his beggar's bowl with scraps
Only so that you might steal his alms
He thought he would forever remain a beggar in this life
He thought he would be a beggar beyond death
And when at the end of his journeys
He came fearfully to your door
You received him with your own garland of flowers.

Will they come back? asked Esha's uncle. They had been gone for half an hour, the skies had darkened since, an eerie light shone through the cracked clouds, will they come back? he asked, his teacup trembling upon his lips. Many years ago his nephew had walked out on an afternoon much like this, married a Nigerian woman, and never come back. The world is full of evil, he said, look at our lives, you have lost your wife, the girl has lost her mother, and I have lost everything.

He wore his old black suit, he had been to the bank that afternoon to discuss his finances. I had thought of looking into the possibility of returning to India, of retiring to a modest villa in the hills somewhere, I could not bear to be in Calcutta of course, he told me.

The bank manager was extremely polite as always, he continued, I remember the days when they were so hideously supercilious, gone are those days, but even as the chap courteously laid out all the possible routes, I knew I could never do it, that frankly I lack the courage to go back home, that I was destined to keel over someday against these damp walls, clawing at the laughing cherubs and gangrened roses. I will fall, and none of you will know until the milkman finds the bottles collecting ominously on the doorstep, the smells of charred lentils and my rotting flesh trickling out slowly through the cracks in the front door.

They walk in silence down the High Street, Yuri Sen stops to buy a pack of cigarettes, Anya picks out a bar of white chocolate and places it on the counter, he smiles and pays, pats her on her head as she unwraps it and hastily starts to nibble on its sweet sticky flesh. Two dachsunds in orange coats run past them, almost tripping her up, she clings to Yuri Sen's arm, a sudden gust of rain forces them to take shelter under the awning of Robert May: Shopfitters. She munches on her chocolate as the rain spits desultorily around her ankles, licks her sticky fingers, and turns her face away from the damp smoke that Yuri Sen blows out of his fine nostrils, he senses her discomfort and turns his face away from her, turns to face the grim length of the street, the shoppers struggling with umbrellas, lowering plastic shields over perambulators and pushchairs, the butcher's assistant hastily gathering up the cartoned eggs, the reduced-price chickens, the greengrocer throwing tarp over his wretched aubergines. These are the colours of my past, thinks Yuri Sen, blowing rings of cold smoke, these are the colours of my past that I have always longed to escape. He remembers how his parents would drag them to the shops on Saturdays, where if they were lucky they were allowed to sit in the car and read, while their parents stocked up for the week, hunted for bargains, and cheap presents for their friends' anniversaries, children's birthdays. If they were lucky they would be left alone to read in the car, he and Luna slumped in the back, Sputnik whining in the front seat and racing his myriad matchbox cars on the dashboard, shut up Sput, Luna would call whenever their brother got carried away, and Sputnik would sulkily sink back into his seat and suck his lips in boredom, but Yuri Sen was always somewhere else, somewhere very far away, in the depths of some jungle writhing upon a carpet of snakes, scaling a frosted cone upon a planet of icecream, or on his belly scratching for coal in a nineteenth-century mine, until his parents returned, their nerves frayed, tempers badly patched, and it was time to help them load the shopping and go back home.

Are you sure they will return? asked Esha's uncle, I did not trust that man, who is he, anyway?

The firstborn of a certain Dr Sen of Dagenham, I replied.

The old man laughs. I was at his daughter's wedding last week, he says. So that is the son who disappeared seven years ago. Apparently he made a brief appearance at the wedding, there was quite a commotion when I arrived, either the groom was missing or the bride was missing, I cannot remember which, but finally they got them both in the same place, and the ceremony was performed, not that I saw any of it, I simply ate and left, as I always do upon these occasions.

Life is full of coincidences, I said.

How can you trust such a man with her? he asked, you should not have let her go with him.

I filled our teacups for a third time, poured in the heavy milk, you will not like this, I said, but she is carrying his child.

He took his tea and drank in one shaky gulp. You are all evil, he said presently, at the end of the day you are all accomplices of some very dark force, it is no wonder that my niece threw herself under a train.

We do not know that she threw herself under the train, I lied.

Of course she did, why else would she have called that woman in Paddington to tell her she was going to jump onto the tracks?

I did not know you read the tabloids, I replied, much less that you believed in any of what they say.

Look, he said, I am going upstairs. When I come down again, I want you gone, you, that poor girl, and that evil being, I want no traces of you left in this house.

This house is my temple, he said, rising from his chair. This house is my sanctuary from evil, this house is my temple, and someday soon it will be my tomb.

They turned into a street at the Turnpike Lane underground station, and walked down the wet pavement, dodging the dog litter and the broken glass. A small red sock intercepted their path at an ominously cheerful angle, Anya dug her hands into the pockets of her overcoat, why is he dragging her around these miserable streets, she wondered, what did he want to tell her, surely that he must leave her, that life has caught up with them now, they are no longer characters in some elaborate charade, simply destitutes, now that they are no longer part of a grand and fragile whim, they must go their own ways, surely this is what he has come to tell her, as kindly as he can, Yuri Sen, a beggar in fine clothing, surely he has simply come to say goodbye.

They walked past a noisy school, in the throes of closing for Christmas, children streaming out of the gate like multi-coloured lozenges, the tinny froth of their merriment clumped in Anya's throat, she rushed hurriedly past, crossed the road dangerously to Downhills Park, stood trembling by the park rails, crisp wrappers chewing at her heels, while Yuri Sen caught up with her.

The light was low now, the naked trees wreathed in the luminiscence of a newly washed sunset, Anya gripped the wet rails and began silently to sob. Yuri Sen stroked her sticky hair, unclenched what was left of the chocolate bar from her hand and threw it to a staring squirrel. I have the money now to come with you to Calcutta, said Yuri Sen.

But she only sobbed harder, pressing her head against the rusty rails. I thought you had come to say goodbye, she said.

I have not come to say goodbye, said Yuri Sen.

I still do not understand why, she said, her tears flowing fast.

I will never leave you, he said resolutely, always remember

this, I will never leave you, not unless you tell me to go.

But you do not love me, she said.

I will never leave you, said Yuri Sen.

The Book
of Brass

❋

I was asleep when the rain came, spitting upon the portals of afternoon slumber, the rain, in sizzling baconsweat, fell against the cracked shutters and I woke. It was only the first day of rain, she stood on the long verandah, the spray beading the distended marble of her belly, she stood in the virgin smell of the hungry garden, the thickness of wet weed fast upon her tongue, she stood in the shadowed kitchen, unshod, and pressed her ankles to the swollen earthenware jugs, still full of old water, her endless fingers thin against the paper print of her summer blouse, riding high against her sweet swollen breasts. I gave her my arm, remembering how I had lifted her, only a few months ago, a wisp of a girl, I had helped her down a grassy mountain slope, Yuri Sen watching scornfully as I slung her silver laughter about my neck and descended breathful from the heady heights. I gave her my arm now to help her rise from the moist floor, from among the jars of strenuous pickle, nectar to her fretful senses, she buried her silky head upon my chest, will it never end, she wailed, this rain, will it never end?

That this fragile cage of bone might be prison to another eager life seemed beyond belief, her soft young breasts lay piled in shock upon the taut exaggeration of her flesh, her lips beating back the gall of her unhoused gut, the gentle hips quivering like a flower overbloomed, and night rushing ragged through her wide undrinking eyes.

And the rain would not end, the rain that had come like gentle balm at first, to wash the wounds of the cracked pavements, soothe the peeling shutters of this decaying villa, rain that had fallen first like a mother's joy from the skies, would turn into a steady and indifferent downpour, lasting for days. Will it never end? she asked, her ankles crossed upon the patched footstool, watching the rainwater drip through the cracked ceiling into rusty kerosene tins, she dug her nails into the old leather of the easy chair, that same chair where, many years ago, Esha's grandfather had sat and lowered his glasses to scrutinise me, so you are Promothesh, are you? I nodded, clutching my cloth satchel nervously. She tells me you are a genius, he had croaked in English. That was the winter of our first year in college, my first visit to this house, we sat and revised Organic Chemistry at the dining-room table, and a small young servant boy had brought us coffee, my first taste of coffee, in hollowed stainless-steel mugs, thick with boiled milk and sugar. Years later you would addict me to espresso, Alexandra Vorobyova, cup after cup I have drained with you at those unfriendly Queensway cafés, regurgitating the details of my past, you took notes in a small out of date diary. I have a feeling this will be a most fulfilling exercise, you said, after our first session, raising your eyes from your notebook to meet mine, lustsweet from caffeine and nostalgia, go home, you said gently, it is late, Esha will be waiting up for you.

Indeed she was, is it going well? she asked, in a voice badly weeded of pain.

Marvellously well, I replied, except that it makes me dreadfully homesick, makes me wish we had never left Calcutta.

But then you would never have met Alexandra, said Esha, and the story of your life would have drifted unsung, just another thread in the spindle of time, just another thin chord in a tropical storm, just another bellow in the blacksmith's forge . . .

Which is all I ever wanted it to be, I cried fiercely.

I do not believe you, said Esha quietly, why, then, did you turn the garage into a laboratory, why, if you had not a secret taste for the kitchens of hell, did you turn that innocent garage into a laboratory?

Why indeed, but who cares now, but to thank God for it, as we move the gramophone, and some of the old books into the old garage, the only part of the house that has escaped bitter desuetude. In converting it into a laboratory, we had cleaned it of its tropical sores and gangrene, replastered and reinforced, and so it stands, alone and robust, while the rest of the house cracks and falls, under the mute rain, peeling now from the sky in faceless sheets, and sowing deep dissension into the substances of these walls, which cancer and crumble, these old walls, and the rain bleeds through, splits into rivulets, running races to the Persian carpet, where Anya lies, her head upon the patched footstool. You must get up, we coax her, soon the carpet will be soaked through. I lead her to my bedroom, where a blue tarp has been spread over the four posters of our old bed, that once had held the four quiet corners of frothy mosquito net that Esha would tiptoe to hang, every night, tuck evenly around, and slip in with a book, wait for me to wake her, late, and wound her flesh with the excitement of my chemical excursions. First the smaller triumphs, I have done it, I have distilled glycerol, I would gasp upon her sleepsodden lips. And then the grander schemes, all fruiting slowly and steadily, I would lay each sweet success upon the grace of her thickening breasts, and the following evening she would record each manoeuvre in painstaking detail, as I recounted my methods and results. You must not neglect your own work, I told her, this is more important, she replied, sometimes I get tired of numbers, she confessed, shoving her unfinished thesis into a boxfile, and we would climb into the mosquito nets, lie together in delicious exhaustion. It is only the smaller successes that are truly delectable, the first prize in elocution, the inspired late cut, the best words suddenly in the best order, such was the meter of our comfort, as we lay in each other's arms in the humid dark, and yet, I could feel, within her satisfaction, the small hard whispers of a vaster paradox, there within the contours of her soft ear upon my cheek lay an echo of infinity, her fingers pressed upon my temples with the insistence of seashell, patterned with the secrets of the deepest oceans.

It was a month of salt, she said, I would wake to the lazy strokes of the hall clock, shake my limbs free of stale sleep, fling my nightdress into the washbasket, and rush to splash water on my face, the water would make maps of strange worlds upon the bathroom floor, and life would seem merely a blueprint for some vastly grander scheme.

Tell me the truth, asks her mother, as we drag a heavy trunk to staunch the flow of mud from a flapping door, tell me, how did she really die?

She fell in front of a train, I tell her, I am not lying to you.

Were you there? she asks.

I shake my head.

Has it ever struck you, asks her mother, tears running down her rainwet cheeks, do you ever think, Promothesh, that she might have jumped?

What earthly reason would she have to jump? asks Yuri Sen wickedly, appearing suddenly out of the gloom, wrapped to his chin in his long black cape. I turn away and find myself staring at our reflections in a veiny mirror, he could be my shadow, in this mist, a black figure in my wake, my doppelgänger, Yuri Sen, perish the thought.

Suddenly, the phone rings, the phone, marooned upon the sideboard in the dining room, the phone emits a few fossilised peals, stops, and then shudders awake again with a long etherised scream. Yuri Sen, hands over his ears, wades through the mess of floating books and china, to answer the phone, it's like being in a fucking Tarkovsky film, he yells, reaching for the receiver, it's for you, he tells me.

It is my father, brimming with self-congratulation at having achieved the connection, near impossible, he explains, in times of rain, he is phoning from a neighbour's flat, for their telephone has been out of order for many months now. How are you holding up? my father asks, do you have enough rations? They say this may go on yet for a few more days.

The house is falling down, I explain, there is water everywhere.

Why you insist on staying in that haunted house, I do not know, my father mutters, we have had no problems, just a bit of the old damp, and some bad sore throats . . .

Rather this, I think to myself, this consummate decay, this feudal disaster, than the mucid comfort of their rainproof flat, the kerosene sweat and the lemon soap, wet clothes hanging the length of the corridor, and the smell of bored children, kicking their heels in the damp air. I had been to see them only once in the three months since we had arrived, my mother cried to see me, fried my eggs just as I had once liked them, thick in mustard oil, they asked few questions, only as I got up to leave, my father asked, so you will not be staying with us? It was easier, I explained, to stay where I was, I had two young people with me, the girl was pregnant, I had promised her mother I would look after her, I told my perplexed parents. It is a strange life that you lead now, remarked my father, I can see that we have very small roles to play in it, but come and see us when you can.

See if you can find some way to get here, his rainmuffled voice suggests, laden with static, if all of you can somehow float your way across to this part of town.

Rather this, I think to myself, rather to drown in the crumbled mess of plaster and gilt, to breathe my last upon a bed of cracked leather, than to dissolve slowly in the fennel fumes of their last supper, to lose my final consciousness to the fizz and crackle of their television set, better this watery grave, the telephone line sighs and splutters, goes dead, I replace the receiver in its prehistoric cradle, we are running out of drinking water, calls Yuri Sen, from the kitchen, but his voice is scattered by a sudden great wind that ripples the water, it eddies in fascinating swirls around the heavy legs of the dining table, on one of its many claws, my toes had touched for the first time the flesh of a woman, hardly then but a girl, my toes had grazed her ankle, and withdrawn in delicious agony, many years ago, it is such a detail that shudders now beneath these waters, as a great wet wind tears through the house, lifting the tarp off our wedding bed, and blowing it far, over the balcony, onto a mango tree. Anya shifts and moans, shakes off the sodden bedclothes, Yuri Sen covers her with his cape, the mattress is soaking, he announces, we might as well move her to the garage, it's the only safe place.

He helps her rise, eases her feet into sandals, and propels her slowly, under a tattered umbrella, into the hall, and out through the kitchen, towards the garage, standing smugly in a sea of mud, inside we find the cowkeeper who brings us our daily milk, crouching beside a wet calf, let it stay, pleads Anya, let the poor creature stay. Esha's mother comes in with a few dry sheets, all the mattresses are soaked through, she wails, what are we to do? I have some dry straw, says the cowkeeper, in my cowshed, there should still be some dry straw. The rain has let up a little, I wade with him outside the gates, past the melted slums, to his cowshed, crushed mainly to mud, but yes, there is straw, dry and fragrant in my arms, it takes two trips to make a decent bed, we spread clean sheets, and Anya sinks gratefully into its hold. Esha's mother brings tea, and old sugar biscuits, remembers the chipped mug for servants and sales-men to serve a warm cuppa to the cowkeeper, who sips gratefully, slips his sugar biscuit into a fold of his loincloth, for his children, perhaps, or perhaps to eat later, when his hunger is keener still than that which already gnaws within. We sit and sip our tea, the rain has almost ceased, but an ominous luminiscence bathes the skies, and with the first crack of thunder comes her first spasm, the blind call of an unborn child, eager to make its way into a still wetter world.

Dark whiplengths of caramel rain come chasing towards me

as I walk into the flood, with only my umbrella to tell me where the waters are at their deepest, where the manholes gape like toothless vipers, waiting for their prey. I make my way past the sea of slum towards the encroaching mass of middle-class dwellings, where perhaps a doctor might be found. These had been fields, and hyacinth ponds, for the house had crouched on the very edge of this narrow city, when I first set foot within its hallowed walls, there was only the smell of autumn reeds then, blowing in from the wide fields, and the etched symphony of her elbow ploughing the silence, as she brought together her fingers, and carved a column of air, fullerenes, Esha told me, were hollow hexahedron tubes of carbon, as if I did not know, but where was my mind but upon the stiff curve of her elbow, already I was content to pass the rest of my life among the arrogance of women, their concentrated devotion, now like iron, now like sand, so utterly cleaved from its obscure object, so firmly complete within itself, so easily eschewed.

Soaked beyond the skin, I take brief shelter in a broken tea stall, sit under a scrap of roof to catch my breath, and find myself face to face suddenly, upon the mudbled walls, with a few wilted colour photographs of an intimate family gathering probably in some expatriate dwelling in the States, obviously intercepted in the post. Such photographs as Esha might have sent to her mother, of our London flat, of Sir Percival's lovely garden, and perhaps among these one of you, Alexandra Vorobyova, a vibrant tableau of you and I, enswirled by our neonate passion, you and I, trapped in time against one of Sir Percival's urns, having submitted reluctantly to Esha's frenzied urge to record every moment of our lives, dig her compass deep into the arc that stretched to her death. She would have had someone photograph her fall, film her terrible end in grave and coarse detail. While I scratched in my seabeds for bright memories to offer at your feet, she was coding her despair in the truculence of light, engraving her pain upon the fatuous gloss. Those that she had sent her mother might easily have ended up here, upon these walls, gnawed by the heat and the rain, some urchin's loot, lovingly tacked onto these dying walls, for rickshawpullers and busdrivers to dream by, one of Esha's photographs, as the only one of you that I still possess, with the red of your brilliant hair poisoning the sunlight, while I stand beside you, chewing an arm of my spectacles, your long green scarf draped by the wind over the urn, stretches tight across its belly of stone, for Esha had insisted that we pose for her in that hideous moment of outbranching desire, an act of odd despair on her part, it is the only photograph that I have of you now. Much of the time she preferred to photograph nature, glutting her sorrow upon the rich conceit of autumn, a feast to starve each branch, endlessly she roamed the ephemeral grandeur of the London parks with her heavy camera, wedding present from her brother, one of our preciousmost possessions, we brought it with us to London, back to the land of its birth, where it would become an ally of pain, she would roam the streets with its heavy weight around her neck. Every time she clicked it was like a whip falling across her back, she would have recorded her own death, I am sure, in harsh black and white, if it had been possible, instead she telephoned an old woman in a Paddington council flat, a sequence of numbers picked out of the air, heavy as diamonds upon her fingers, as one by one they came and vanished, and her death, once grand in its anonymity, gripped its belly, and watched the stuffing drizzle, she dialled and pronounced her fate to a fading mind with a fondness for jam tarts, an old woman in an orange cardigan, whose daughter coaxed her to give her story to the papers. Yuri Sen had been furious, can they not leave her tragedy alone? he cried, slapping the hoary tabloid upon the dining table, where I sat, my grief strewn like a broken bag of potatoes about my feet, Yuri Sen buried his head in his hands and began to sob, gently you eased the paper out from under his long elbows, she lives just round the corner, you said. Months later, you would visit the old woman, armed with jam tarts and your notebook, your flaming hair tucked away into an unruly bun. You returned, laden with the last traces of her life, the sausage smells where Esha's last words had drifted, already ghostly, already steeped in the brine of an undigested afterlife. You flung yourself into an armchair, unpinned your hair, and turned your glassgreen eyes to me, and confessed, I went to see her, the old woman that Esha called before she died, I went to see her.

I was sitting by the window, smoking quietly, my new plans to save the world scattered around me. In those months since Esha's death I had given myself wholly and completely to my work, and for the first time in a long time, a glimmer of fruition seemed hidden among the mass of numbers, the lozenge-coloured graphs. Once again I was a dreaming scientist, the careless magician who would make grass from gold, suddenly her death seemed distant and small, a necessary sacrifice, an invited martyrdom, her meagre role in a grand cause. And now only the narrowing tendrils of her fate clung to you, cobwebbed within the smells of leaking gas and old bacon, I took a handful of your hair and crushed it to my lips, and you, shaken by my sudden boldness, pulled me down from my window seat, and made frenzied love to me, one swift movement gliding into another, as your tongue thundered new upon my palate, and the emptiness of your thighs creasing like a question mark over my body, shrouded in loose linen, my blood funnelled and split into a thousand rivers, while you gasped and dug your knees into the injured carpet, I fell like a dead bird into a bottomless crevice in a field of old rock.

And later as we sat, swallowing odd daylight, your jawbone gently nested against my shoulder blade, my mind circling the sad skies of reason, seeking to empower my desire with logic, struggling to enslave the arrogance of your satisfaction, I felt myself slip once more into the salty grasp of a woman's ambition, the petalled loop of that concentrated urge to gently squeeze all but the best out of life, I felt myself wandering once more between the chalk columns of a woman's dream, a small sorry figure, aching for a cigarette and a good book, I felt myself sinking into the rich gravel of a woman's quest, born of aeons of crushed hope, you shifted your cheek against my backbone, we must finish your autobiography, you said.

With your cheek in the hollow embrace of my shoulderbones, you began to speak of your past, of your first evening in New York, the small room in the Brooklyn apartment where you had been told to rest, while your parents chattered excitedly outside with their friends, reunited after years of waiting, and you, alone, in your room, thumbed numbly through magazines that you could not read, you were eleven years old, utterly ignorant of the English language, you felt, you said, like a young girl who has inherited a wide and rocky farm, where she knows one day she will strike oil, but for the moment sits upon her dusty suitcase, gazing into the distance, the relentless horizon, the hard blue sun. So you told me with your cheek upon my bowed back, and I stared at my useless hands, that still did not dare to stroke your hair, to caress your flesh in the tender aftermath of passion, I would never seize you, as Juan Gorrion would, only a few months later, while you pleaded with a refugee child who had hidden himself in a tall laundry basket, Juan Gorrion would wrap his arms about you from behind, drop the lid upon the poor child and impale you in *Decameron*esque delight, Juan Gorrion, master of a thousand stratagems, man of many lies, whom you would follow to the bowels of this earth, never to return.

I peel a scabied photograph off the soft wall, and under the pressure of this movement, the remains of the shack fall, it heaves and crumples into a mud mass, and the rain syringes and darkens upon me, I begin to make my way once more towards the cluster of dim lights in the distance, in search of a doctor. Dark melted forms move towards me, it is the cowkeeper, and his wife, I came to fetch her, he explains, gesturing towards his wife. The pains are getting worse, he says, have you not found a doctor yet? I am finding it hard to navigate in the rain, I explain, wretched with guilt at having tarried in the crumbling tea shack, it is getting dark, sympathises the cowkeeper, you had better hurry. They stagger on, pushing against the rain, while I, moving in the opposite direction, am pushed, gently guided by the rainforce, towards the muted carnival of lights, the limits of conurbation, thickening daily with new growth, a weedy plot suddenly sprouting a new white block of flats, new floors added upon old homes, it is all so much changed that I can barely recognise any of it, for since my return I have always taken the alternative route to the city, in my eagerness to avoid this faceless urban spillage, I have always taken the short cut through the golf course, to the auto-rickshaw stand by the old mosque, or a little further down the road to the bus stop where Esha would stand and wait for me, while we were still college students, if there was something worth seeing at the nearby new cinema. It was there that we saw *Love Story*, and I had wondered then, glancing sidelong at her face in the heady luminiscence, how would I go on if she died, if some strange dream would consume her from within, how would I go on? In the interval, we would buy a chocolate bar, split it neatly down the middle, I would munch my half quickly, but she would keep hers for a while, taking small bites, the first time I kissed her, in that empty hall, I shared her mouth with a lump of chocolate, there, I said to her, strangely articulate after my bold feat, now I have had more than my fair share, she laughed and broke off a piece and pushed it into my mouth, I kissed the tips of her fingers, the credits fell, and we walked out into the bald sunshine, afraid to meet each other's eyes. They have painted the building a practical grey now, to match the pollution, these days they only show commercial Hindi films, and the courtyard is full of narrow-waisted young men, smoking harsh cigarettes, I pass them often on my way to town, for that is my preferred route, rather their foul indolence than the wretched middle-class disharmony of these new dwellings where I wander now in the aching darkness, lit only by the tremulous cones of kerosene lamps, for most of the power lines are down, a few generators splutter and die, and the streets are empty as rivers, where I wander in the now frivolous rain, in the hope of finding a doctor, someone who will be willing to walk back the quarter mile to the crumbled villa, to the stolid garage, where a young girl screams in the madness of new life, Esha's mother holds her temples, the cowkeeper's wife boils water on the kerosene stove, her husband soothes the frightened calf, and Yuri Sen stands drenched at the gate, waiting for me to return.

I grope blindly past inundated doorways, locked gates, dead doorbells, I find the house of our old family physician, buried between two eager fivestoreyed blocks, the rusty gate still sports a peeling plaque bearing his various degrees, I push it open and wade to the door, bang hard, and am eventually answered by a muffled voice, it is their crippled maid, she will not open the door, they have gone away, she tells me, their son came and took them away, a few days ago, to his Southern Avenue flat, there they would at least be dry, the ageing physician and his wife. How could I have expected him to walk back to our house, anyway, I would have had to carry him, crooked and soaked, only to watch him minister half-senile to the birthpangs of the girl, your daughter, blue in childbirth, whom you left behind, to follow a cheap puppetmaker into the glory of doom, the heat of senseless sacrifice.

I pick my way through the Jurassic slime back to the gate, whose rusty jaws the wind has fiercely locked while I was communing with the maid. Can you help me? I call out to an old man wandering past with a shrivelled umbrella and a large plastic bag. He hesitates, sets down his load, and unclenches iron from iron with a sharp twist of his hand, do you know where I can find a doctor? I ask him.

He shakes his head numbly, and bends pick up his bag, through the grubby tearstained plastic I can see a rabbit, obviously dead, stretched long in rigour, they keep digging him up, the old man complains, I buried him the day before yesterday in a shoe box, in the morning I looked out of my flat window, and there he was, dug up, flung onto the garbage heap, I rescued him, washed him, and buried him again, and this afternoon, I saw they had cast him on the rubbish heap again, by then it was raining, and the water was already ankle-deep, I have been searching for hours now for a place to bury him, do you know where I might find some dry ground? he asks me.

Perhaps the roundabout near the Post Office? I suggest, wiping oily ribbons of rain from my face.

But how will I place flowers on his grave if I bury him upon the roundabout? he asks, his dark eyes darting in his fleshy face like a pair of frightened deer. He was fond of flowers, in the last few months of his life, he refused to eat anything but the hearts of marigolds, at least it made his incontinence fragrant, the old man says, tears streaming down his bristly cheeks.

They keep digging him up, he says, looking suddenly over his shoulder, as if they might be following him.

They will get tired of it, I console him, your perseverance will overwhelm their malice, surely, I say, words geysering through the pulp of my thoughts, he will have a decent burial, I am sure of it, I tell him.

Do you think they might have poisoned him? the old man asks, do you think they might have bribed the housepainter to mix arsenic into the whitewash, they would have known that a rabbit would chew at the walls, would they not?

Poison? I ask absently, surely not? And my words are caught in a sea of filth, as a furious gust of sour wind everts my umbrella, and my balance is lost, I fall, and with me falls the old man, the rabbit slipping from his grasp, and vanishing into the vast waters. The currents drag him quickly away in his plastic cocoon, the old man does not attempt to follow, merely stares into the murk, wiping rainslime from his unruly eyebrows, he's gone, he says simply, as the ghostly glimmer of what could be the rabbit's shroud, bobs up in the distance and floats away, his was a watery grave, he pronounces suddenly in English, his was a watery grave.

A hand falls upon his shoulder, his nephew, carrying a torchlight, come home, he says gently, and turning to me he expresses gratitude for having taken care of his uncle.

How have I helped? I ask, I could not even rescue the rabbit.

His was a watery grave, repeats the uncle.

Do you know where I can get a doctor? I ask the nephew.

My daughter is an intern at the National, he tells me, perhaps she can help, where is the patient?

And so it came to pass that your daughter was delivered of a healthy pinkfaced child by a rather serious young woman, her glasses blue with steam, who had waded with me from her father's home to our crumbling mansion, her white sari twisted with rain about her knees. We had arrived not a moment too soon, and the cowherd's wife had wept with relief to see us, and Esha's mother with her hand upon Anya's head, had quite unexpectedly made the sign of a cross. The baby was placed upon clean sheets on a pile of fresh hay, while Yuri Sen knelt bewildered by fatherhood at her side, with one hand restraining the curious calf, for the cowherd and his wife had gone back to fetch some lentils and rice from their meagre stores for our dinner. The young doctor stayed to share our saltless meal, tending to Anya, who still groaned and muttered under wetfelted dreams, waking now and then to glance at her child, with an almost sorrowful tenderness, a milkswollen disquiet that drenched us all in deep and terrible compassion for the helpless being, I raised my eyes to the ravaged skies, where stars, stripped clean, shone without mercy in the deep night.

For a few months there was a joy that could only be the joy of heaven, if one were to put a name to it, a joy so pure and subtle, so steady and windless, so small-pebbled and yet so vast that if one were to have to condense it into a few vitreous syllables, it would certainly be heaven, where even our pocket Lucifer would have a place, Yuri Sen, now turned tiller of the soil, he did not trust market vegetables, they dip them in coloured water, he complained, we will grow our own, at least for the child, proclaimed Yuri Sen. And so while I eased back into my lecturing job, Yuri Sen turned the wreckage of the back garden into a small farm, he even had a few chickens, but they never appeared to lay any eggs, the mice must be stealing them, grumbled Yuri Sen. I would come home from college to find him bent over some horny patch, desperately prodding the knots of madder with a rusty spade, while Anya rocked her child in an old swing that had been used to soothe the infant Esha, many many years ago. We had managed to reclaim most of the house, it stood bandaged and plastered, smelling strongly of new whitewash, wonderfully bare, for much of the sodden furniture had been carried over to the garage where it was hoped that the horsehair and the coir would gradually dry without becoming home to a thousand lichens, armies of fungus, and all manner of small beasts to graze such new pastures. Every morning Esha's mother would sprinkle her precious chairs with fungicides and pesticides, until her wrinkled fingers came to be permanently dusted with green salts, and her proud nails filmed with oily residues whose smells we would find in our rice and lentils, all for your rotten chairs, Yuri Sen would fume, syringe your sprung mattresses with kerosene if you will, but spare us these saturated miseries. And quietly the old woman would cover the scorned food and return to the kitchen to boil some eggs for our lunch, and there stirring aimlessly at the boiling water, her despair would be outstung by memories rushing back to fill the absurd outlines of her life as matron of this paradisic household. She would remember how her daughter, in the lyric meridian of her love for me, had thrown herself into cookery, humming delicately as she prepared Prawn Tom Yum one night, and a Kashmiri Biryani the other, as if her creativity and intellect might be subdued finally by the challenge of domesticity, as if the steam of boiled spinach upon her brow might soften the stern architecture of her thoughts, that her mind rushing towards the stars might be weighted down with baked eggs. So her mother had watched in sorrow as Esha tried to tame her soul with exercises of cookery, and yet all too quickly, it became terribly effortless, like all else that she put her hand to, it acquired an insubstantiality, a buoyancy, curled like a comma into the phrases of her life, where she might have welcomed a heavier punctuation, a few globs of mercury, if only so that when I touched her, I might feel that I held more than a spiralling intellect, a restless core of energy, a perfect lattice of light.

One morning, while hunting through her grandfather's Botany texts, he stumbles across Esha's thesis, Yuri Sen, searching a cure for potato blight, pulls out from the dusty embrace of two motheaten monographs on runner beans, her forgotten thesis, hastily typed, badly bound, and with this epigraph, beautifully scripted upon the first page: *the flower says I am eternally beholden to earth, but let me forget that I have been conceived in dirt, for I am pure*, she was made for the stars, sobs Yuri Sen, and you threw a wet tea towel over her dreams, he curses me, all afternoon he pores over her thesis, the plight of his potatoes forgotten. At first his appreciation is purely sensuous, the equations written in her flowing yet exact hand, graceful, upright, burning with dignity and pain, a whaleboned universe, at first his fingers merely stray along its stern lines, and then the floodgates open and he is drowned in the ecstasy of comprehension, the corsetlaces tighten about his being and he is lifted into the regions of her consciousness that she so longed to leave at times, and yet could never abandon. He roams the sculpted gardens that had become her bitter and permanent home, the long avenues that she would have gladly escaped for a more voluptuous wilderness, she had been cursed with a lack of chaos, never does he feel this more keenly than now, Yuri Sen, mired in bookdust, his thoughts forming strange crystals within their narrow casts.

He remembers how once he had dropped in, late one evening, to our Bayswater flat, and found her alone, drinking sweet wine, an oily Monbazillac that he took one sip of, and no more, I could have written his autobiography, she said suddenly to him, unnaturally flushed, for I was, at that very moment entwining my fingers in yours, in a nearby café, as I spoke achingly of my youth, and you, with your left hand wrote. It is not a sin to be holding hands, is it? I asked you, you shrugged and smiled, and continued to write. We are closing, this waitress announced, and we walked out into the warm night, towards the park, subdued by these first declarations of desire, we walked to the Marble Arch and back again, speaking in low tones of how easy it was to hurt those that we most loved, and I prayed that Esha would be asleep when I returned home. But it was not so, she was awake, wildly awake, feverish with sweet wine, smoking with ease one of Yuri Sen's cigarettes, even though she had never smoked before. I could have written his damned autobiography, she had told him earlier, pressing her dark lips to her glass.

But, my dear, said Yuri Sen, you created him, you had fashioned his biography long before it had been lived. Can you deny, my dear, that in him you set out to create the man of your dreams, knowing that none would be your match, unless you made him so?

He does not love me, she said, rolling her wineglass between her palms in rhythmless anguish.

My dear, I imagine he must despise you, had said Yuri Sen, you have twisted his life into improbable candysticks, you have turned his life into a fairground of deceit, you have made him turn gold into grass, when all he ever wanted to do was to chew the cud.

It was I that sent her to her death, thinks Yuri Sen, running his hands across the soured parchment of her oldest dreams, but perhaps she is more at home within the abstraction of eternity, more at ease in the company of the Creator than she was with mere mortals, perhaps she rests within a cave of salt, watching the ink of her thoughts spread in strange shapes across the walls of salt, she was cursed with a lack of unholiness, reasons Yuri Sen, shutting her thesis, never does the purity of her being cut as sharply into his consciousness as now, Yuri Sen, perched within a house of cards, a curious pain growing in his chest.

He diagnosed it first as bronchitis, the old family physician, returned from his son's Southern Avenue flat, where they had been exiled while their bungalow recuperated from the flood, he had returned to his replastered cradle, and resumed his duties, ministering to the odd cold, the sudden rash, the chronic neighbourhood aches, he pressed his old stethoscope to Yuri Sen's downy chest, and clucking softly announced that it was a particularly bad case of bronchitis, prescribed a rainbow of antibiotics, and an Ayurvedic tonic. I have seen you working barechested in the garden at dusk, he scolded, you must be more careful now that winter is approaching.

Indeed there was a slight chill to the evening wind, the strange soapy smell of hope in the air, as the pujas approached, the skeleton of a canopy for the gods grew sturdier in the children's park, while Yuri Sen worsened, his eyes receding further into their orchestral pits, his tongue furzing with an unquenchable thirst, the canopy took on swathes of colour, the idols arrived, chaste in sacking, and the skies stretched taut with the suspense of festivity, while Yuri Sen's condition became progressively more grave. And yet there was a peace within us which could only be the peace of angels, to whom death and sickness are old allies, that they may sit beside a writhing corpse and knit clever mittens, such was our peace, as we sequestered in his sickroom, Esha's mother wiping his hot brow with a damp cloth every few minutes, Anya rocking her child at some distance from its sick father, and I marking pre-puja exams, thoroughly and inexplicably content.

Are you poisoning me? he asked once, as I counted out his capsules, yellow and blue, purple and green, talk about broad-spectrum! I laughed. Are you sure you aren't slowly poisoning me? he asked, Yuri Sen, his fevered mind pulsating to the distant beat of festival drums, wild-eyed idols stirring his brains into porridge with their many limbs, the faulty Sanskrit of the hired *purohits* drifting towards him from the distant mega-phones like snatches of a bad dream. The priest must always have his back to us, insisted Yuri Sen, he must never turn to face us, never should he indicate that we might share his communion with eternity, his vast pain, are you sure you are not poisoning me? asked Yuri Sen. Take your medicine, I urged him gently, pushing the many-coloured capsules past his dry lips. I left a glass of water trembling in his weak hands as I rushed away to answer the doorbell, it was the local puja committee, asking for extra funds, I gave them twenty rupees, they grumbled for more, and while I negotiated with the youths, Yuri Sen extracted the softened capsules from the dry folds of his tongue, and hid them under the mattress, as he did every time, three times a day, when I gave him his medicine, he would keep them in the cleft of cheek and jaw, until he was alone, to spit them out and shove them under his mattress. Sometimes they leaked their bitter contents, their vile spores, that no amount of water and syrup would erase from his tastebuds, but most of the time he managed to extract them still intact, stuff them between the cotton overmattress and the coir undermattress, so that he might sleep, a prince upon peas, secure that my plans to poison him would never meet with any success, though meanwhile he might waste away, consumed by unhindered parasites, his lungsacs slowly filling with water.

Outside the girls gathered, freshly bathed, in their new puja clothes, their hands full of flowers, Anya joined them, in graceful white, to say a prayer for Yuri Sen, sunk in deathly sleep, breathing like a seahorse thrown sideways upon the shore. How is your husband? they asked her, fragrant virgins, their hair oiled into long plaits, how is your husband? they would ask her, and dreamily Anya would reply, he is recovering, but very slowly, for somehow in the mist haze of our miraculous life, we none of us acknowledged his steady decay, Yuri Sen, his bright eyes gleamed with the fires of hell in their cavernous sockets, and still we ignored his condition, he would surely have died, Yuri Sen, if my father had not unexpectedly paid us a visit, and insisted that we move him to hospital. On the final day of festivities, the idols taut with dust, awaiting submersion, my father had arrived with my nephew to collect my respects, so grudgingly given, you should have looked in on us, he complained, your mother is most aggrieved. But we never had much regard for ritual, Esha and I, I reminded him how we would invariably escape to the Himalayan foothills at this time of the year, where between the whitewashed walls of Buddhist monasteries, the smoky incense sour upon my palate, I would experience a nameless pain that seemed to fill and spread beyond the outlines of my being, that I later came to recognise as the ancestor of my yearning for you, speckled with the blood of a thousand dying evenings, and the blue afterlives of a thousand small cake candles extinguished by childbreath, a thousand warm icebergs melting simultaneously around a bewildered whale.

His condition is critical, pronounced my father, with a hand upon Yuri Sen's brow, he must be removed at once to hospital, how could you let this happen to him?

Many years ago he had sold his medical textbooks to buy himself a pair of new sandals for the job that he had taken at the Tax Office, abandoning his medical studies so that his brothers and sisters might eat. You must be better shod, his boss had warned him, it makes a bad impression to be so carelessly attired, and so he had sold his textbooks, ground his last hopes of resuming his medical studies firmly into the dust, and earnestly dedicated himself to civil service, put his brothers through professional schools, arranged reasonable marriages for his younger sisters, married and raised a family of his own. His sons had both disappointed him, especially myself, for I was certainly clever enough to study medicine, but had opted instead for the salt stretches of a purer science, for there was an aura of wizardry about the medical profession that discomfited me. What if I should stray too close to the ineffable membranous secret of life, like the poor chemist Berzelius, who woke one day to find he had distilled urea from common inorganic substances, urea, that he had thought only the processes of life could generate. The division of labour between himself and his Creator thus destroyed, he had stood, I imagined, in his dusty laboratory, and swallowed the vivid fumes in despair. That I too would eventually stub my toes on the thin line between life and unlife I did not know then, I had flatly refused to study medicine, I would rather fill my life with small neat truths than with vast disorderly revelations, I explained to my father, who shook his head in helpless disbelief, you won't even sit for the Joint Entrance exam? he asked incredulously, no, I said, no, never, never, I would really rather die. Indeed, you will, my father replied, with a degree in Chemistry in this job market. And where would I have been now, if I had not married the only daughter of a rich barrister? Nursing an incipient rheumatism perhaps within the cob-webbed walls of a government flat, marking college exams, and cursing myself for not heeding my father's advice, cursing my brother for standing staunchly by my side, he would support me, he had declared, he would not let me turn into the spiritual cripple he had become, he had said with emotion, slaving away at a job he despised. I was to be truly free, he had decided, so that in my freedom perhaps he might slightly catch the lingering scent of his own hopes and dreams. Yet I may have cursed him now for his indulgence, if a schoolmaster's poverty had come to weigh heavy upon my limbs, if the fate that I had courted so defiantly in the first flush of knowledge, had indeed come to be mine.

He is hardly conscious, said my father, laying his hand upon Yuri Sen's fevered brow, how could you have let him deteriorate so.

I went for a taxi while my father made phone calls to find him a hospital bed, Yuri Sen, sunk in stupor, the terrible taxi ride nearly shook the remaining scraps of life out of him. He reached towards a nurse pushing tubes into his arms and called her Esha, for he had remembered suddenly how on the night before her death, he had been to see her, she was drinking white wine, a dreadful Monbazillac, waiting for me to return with my new secrets raw against my lips, he offered her one of his foul French cigarettes, when I came in they were silently smoking, I saw that she inhaled the vile smoke with strange ease, I coughed and smiled and excused myself, hid my trembling soul in layers of hot steam in the small bathroom, while he took her by her shoulders and looked deep into her eyes, tears smarting in his own eyes, the priestess, he said to her, biting his bloodless lips in turn, the priestess must never turn to face her guests, said Yuri Sen.

I sent her to her death, sobs Yuri Sen.

Hush now, I tell him, my hand upon his forehead.

And now you are killing me, he says.

Try to sleep, I tell him.

Kill me quickly if you must, says Yuri Sen.

For his twelfth birthday his father had given him a model of the human viscera, Dr Sen of Dagenham had proudly presented his firstborn with the blood and guts that were to be his livelihood, his mission. His father had not bothered to wrap it in fancy paper, there it was waiting for him on the breakfast table, balancing on its truncated thighs, one half of its thorax merely skinned to show the muscles and veins, the other half brutally flayed to expose a candycoloured heart, one petrified lung lingering lovingly over the smooth diaphragm, and below that the abdomen, flung wide in all its glory, ending in an indeterminate junction with the thighs, and then there was the head, again only half shelled to show the brain, folded like meagrely filled sausage, detachable at its midseam, where a neat solid section would appear if one hemisphere were removed. Yuri Sen sat down in front of his cereal in a daze, he had been hoping for a new bicycle. His father excitedly explained the functions of the various organs, Yuri Sen sat mesmerised not by the curious entrails but by the strange expression on the half side of the mannikin's face that was intact, finely sculpted, supremely indifferent to the rest of his condition, here was human dignity reduced to its essentials, from the stoic arch of the half nose to the cold compelling gaze of the single perfect blue eye, filling his small mind, mocking him. The spell was suddenly broken by his brother, Sputnik Sen, seven years old, pyjama-clad, he rushed in singing 'Happy Birthday', saw the terrible toy, and ran screaming from the room, Sputnik Sen, who would later ask Yuri's permission to take it with him to Stanford, this strange flayed beast, Sputnik Sen would install it in his college room, where his friends would pronounce it a truly cool addition, this gutted apparition, that had scared him witless many years ago, centrepiece at his brother's birthday breakfast, it had been hastily removed for Sputnik's benefit, who crept suspiciously back to his seat, still whimpering. Stop being a baby, their sister said to him, Luna Sen, prim in her school clothes, she handed him a small parcel, Happy Birthday, Yuri, she said, she had saved her pocket money to buy him a small grey hippo, thank you, said Yuri Sen, placing it carefully beside his plate of sausages and scrambled eggs.

I am dying, he told her, I know I am dying.

Anya smiled and shook her head, you will be better soon, she said distantly, placing her hand upon his forehead, your lungs are clear, the doctor said so.

What will you do, if I die? he asks.

You will not die, she says.

But if I do, he asks, not now perhaps, but as I am leaving the hospital, if I am hit by a truck, what will you do?

What nonsense you speak, she chides him.

But if I die, he persists, if I should suddenly pass away, where will you go in this wide world?

Back to my grandparents, I suppose, she says slowly.

And she wonders how it will be, the possibility of his death lodged now like ice within her, his death that she has so long denied, how will it be then to return to Fairhaven, New Jersey, all the girls and boys she knew but never loved now grown and gone away, to college or just away, away as she had, away as she had always wanted to be, so much so that she had never treated them as real, never given them anything that they might have given back to her, that might have been there for her now, if she were to return, to the old house by the sea, the cold grey sea, hardbiting and curled of lip, where her father had first kissed her mother, many years ago, under the light of the cracked tin stars, the first night you had taken him home, Robin Underhill, your radical young British professor, on sabbatical from Oxford, you had taken him home, your new discovery, your latest find, Robin Underhill, your parents found him unbearable, it is as if he is coated in glass, you heard your father say to your mother as she fretted over her burnt stew, I love burnt stew, declared Robin Underhill, nothing like burnt stew, he said, rubbing his hands together in glassfilled glee. That night he kissed you, under the sorry stars, kissed you with an unprecedented Gaelic passion that raised him in one long swoop from the level of your curiosity to the nether tips of your dreams, I could live with you forever, he promised, upon this beach, in a cave of salt, do you not wish, he said suddenly, holding you away, do you not sometimes wish that life could be simple, hopelessly simple, that your only concern might be to feed yourself, to laugh and to sleep in the arms of one you love, do you never wish this? asked Robin Underhill. Never, you replied. He laughed, not ever have I felt the desire for peace, but only in your arms, contained from the turbulence of our times, do I long suddenly, like an overexcited child finding its head suddenly against pillow, to plunge swiftly and without thought into sleep, only with you, he confessed, do I ever crave that it will end in primroses and parsnips, for how else could I live with you forever if some part of me did not stop thirsting for new pastures, if some part of me did not find comfort in grass instead of seeking gold?

I would return to my grandparents, said Anya sadly, if you died, I would go back to my grandparents.

I cannot move my legs, said Yuri Sen.

I am dying, I know I am dying, said Yuri Sen.

The paralysis will wear off, I told him, the doctor has said so.

I feel like a hut upon fowl's legs, said Yuri Sen, my body is heavy, and my legs are weak, I cannot feel my legs, he weeps, what have you done to me? asks Yuri Sen.

It will all be alright, I attempt to console him, I have not slept at all myself all night by his side, think of your body as having gone on a pilgrimage, I tell him.

Call the doctor, says Yuri Sen, I cannot breathe.

Think of your body as having departed on a precious pilgrimage, I tell him, from which it will return cleansed, purified, whole, unspoilt.

I am choking, he pleads, you are killing me, call the doctor, please.

Think of your body as numbed by ice, walking for miles over treacherous tundra, a hard time you have had of it, your camels have died, and yet at the end, you will emerge transmogrified, exultant, your limbs streaming with morning music, think of it so.

Now I perceive your scheme, says Yuri Sen, you wish not to kill me, but to effect a metamorphosis, there would be your true victory, to forge my darkly preserved conscience into silver shapes beyond my reason, to pickle my senses into a salty sensual mass, that is your prerogative, I can see it now, says Yuri Sen, between shallow tortured breaths.

Think of your spirit as sluiced by snow, its firm crystals rubbing you raw, so that new skin might grow where the old wounds have gone, think of time as shedding anew from your familiar sores, rise and face this new century, I tell Yuri Sen.

I cannot breathe, he pleads.

Before being was nothingness, I tell him, my hand firm upon his brow, through nothingness you must pass before you can truly be.

What has my life been but nothingness? he protests, momentarily diverted.

You have cluttered the empty space of your existence with many useless things, I tell him, my fingers pressing upon his temples, what you need is a space of pure nothingness, which is what you are about to enter, from which you will emerge, I promise you, the better for it, the softer of spirit, the sterner of mind . . .

Yuri Sen began to choke, I rang for the night nurse.

We will have to perform a tracheostomy, the doctor told me, I'm afraid it will ruin his career.

What career? I asked.

I thought he was a male model, said the doctor.

I stared at him horrified.

No more open-shirted advertisements, said the doctor sadly.

Will he survive? I asked.

God willing, the doctor replied.

Yuri Sen winced.

For three months he lay, trapped within himself, Yuri Sen, chained by the iron of his own inert muscles to his bed, confined within his own cage of nerves, his heart pumped, his blood sang, his brain beat like waves of salt against the prison of his skull, his dark eyes bored us with their sentience, like time without space, his eyes.

What would I give that he might live? thought Anya, not my child, but certainly myself, though I hardly still care for him in the way I did, the fever has passed. I could cheerfully spend the rest of my life without him, yet I would sacrifice myself to deliver him of his condition, most certainly I would, perhaps that is where true fulfilment lies, in giving yourself for one you no longer desire.

The child thrived, began to take solids, mainly a sort of tomato broth that Esha's mother cooked for her, that many a time I was forced to eat when she would not, the young woman who had delivered the child had provided the recipe, it was truly vile. The young doctor came often to see us now, for her medical examinations were over, she would reassure us that Yuri Sen would recover, in time, she said, it may take a long time, wiping her glasses as they steamed over from the vapour of the tomato broth, put some honey in it, she suggested, making a face as she tasted it.

We took the child to the hospital so that he might see her, flesh of his flesh, if that might give him the strength to live, Yuri Sen. She gurgled and cooed, smiled at his frozen face, his dark eyes, sunk in their lignified pits, but alive as the trembling horizons of a tigress stalking her next hunt.

There must be something I can do, thought Anya, some private ritual that will be revealed to me only in the innermost recesses of my concentration. His gaze met hers, locked with it for a few grateful seconds, then passed beyond the territories of her imagination.

I will pray for you, she pledged, I will pray for you as I never have, not since the day, five years ago, when I plucked up enough courage to refuse to attend Synagogue. Her grandmother had shrugged and told her, this comes as no surprise to me, shut her door quietly but firmly, kicking aside a white shoe. Many years ago you had done the same, with more force and passion, crushed their dreams and aspirations, hardly fledged in this New World, scorned their beliefs, taken bacon with your breakfast, milk with your supper, brought home an Englishman whose breath smelled of polythene, married him with his child already in your belly. Where are you now? they wonder sitting under the spring elms, it is almost a year since you phoned or wrote, all they have had is a stream of postcards from India, from their dutiful granddaughter who claims that you are on a mission, that you will contact them when you return. When your father dies of a stroke in March, your mother has nowhere to phone but Sir Percival's, where Blake politely takes the message, but confesses to be clueless as to your whereabouts.

One morning Anya wakes to despair, what if he should remain paralysed all his life, she wonders, what if their lives should be reduced to endless anticipation, a thin thread of false hope. Will she like a mariner's widow hold off her weeds for indefinite years, beyond when he is declared dead by deed rather than by fact, will her child have to live with a fossil for a father, never knowing any other but this eeled mass of intellect, writhing within its seamless carapace. But the child is hardly aware of this monstrous tension, she smiles and babbles away at Yuri Sen as she would to any living creature, he is to her as the noonday sun, immutable, distant, terrible and nourishing, the black eyes silently watch her grow, she does not resent their disquiet any more than she resents the silence of the universe.

That morning she takes the child alone to visit Yuri Sen, in his third month of immobility, the taxi breaks down on Anwar Shah Road, it takes a while before another yields to her request, she reaches the hospital exhausted and flushed, the child withered by heat whimpering in her arms. Yuri Sen has his eyes closed, he keeps them closed now more often than not, she sits quietly by his side rocking the child to sleep, the air feels cheap, as if it has been cooled over dirty ice, and cut into thin strips by the noisy overhead fan, she looks at her arms, speckled like old toast, her hair damp and dull, she feels his eyes upon her, and senses a strange disgust, you look awful, she can hear him say, you look bloody awful, why don't you just go on back to Fairhaven, New Jersey, and leave me to die in peace.

She closes her eyes and fights back her tears, perhaps she should return, perhaps it is time to call an end to this strange chain of events. Perhaps it is time that she conceded that she was not cut out for this sort of life, admitted defeat, as her mother had always hoped she would – you, my dear, would never want to live my life – her mother had told her once – you must find a sweet young man, and bake him cakes and chocolate bunnies – her mother had not been pleased to hear that she had stopped going to Synagogue – what makes you think you have the strength to give up religion? – her mother had asked – there is a lifetime out there to be lived, you think you will be able to manage without God?

The child stirs, Anya opens her eyes to find a stranger in a cream-coloured Nehru suit squatting beside them making funny faces at the baby. It is his child? he asks, motioning towards the supine Yuri Sen. Anya nods. He asks, you are the mother? She nods again and sighs.

We think he is in a trance, the stranger tells her, looking fondly at Yuri Sen, we think he is in a very deep and holy trance, from which he will emerge a saint.

Anya lowers her eyes, for they are swimming again with tears.

Many holy men have meditated thus, the stranger continues, in the days of yore anthills would grow around them, as they sat for years and fasted and concentrated, this is *sadhana* as we have never seen it, he says, spreading his hands wide over Yuri Sen's petrified body.

Anya begins to weep now, holding the child close, she drowns her small head in tears.

You must not cry, the man tells her, it is true that when he wakes he may no longer have any use for you, he will be free after all of all earthly bonds, but he will be a very holy man, a very very holy man.

Anya dries her tears with a corner of Yuri Sen's bedsheet, stands up and walks past him, out of the ward, into the throbbing heat, the sunlight splaying her thoughts into bleeding butterflies. Cars come and go, there is not a free taxi in sight, the child is limp with heat in her arms, has placed her damp hot head upon her shoulder in a dumb resignation that Anya finds hard to bear, I am torturing her, she thinks, I am not fit to mother her, and what am I doing here anyway, I should be in college, studying Comparative Literature and Creative Writing, fretting over my finals for this semester, licking the salt off rimmed Margaritas rather than the perimeter of my ragged mouth, perhaps I should return to my grandparents, unload another daughter's daughter upon them to bring up, while I find a new life, oh, for the coolness of a starched pillow, the shade of a crumbling elm, the heavenly surface of an ice-cold can of Coke against my cheek.

And suddenly he is by her side again, the man in the cream Nehru suit, he smiles and a gold tooth glints, my driver will take you home, he says, you will never find a taxi at this time of day, just tell my driver where you want to go. Gently he guides the dazed Anya into a blue Ambassador, shuts the door, and stoops to tell her, through the window, we will keep an eye upon your husband, you must not worry, just tell the driver where to take you.

We will be watching him, he reassures her, we will be waiting for him to wake.

Later he told us it was the multitude of smells that created for him a most unbearable tapestry, differentiating constantly into finer and finer threads within his caged mind, he became exquisitely sensitive to the change of the proportion of water in the hospital detergent, the rhythmic alterations of the smell of a malarial fever, the phases of pox, the deepening stench of burn in a victim apparently recovered but festering inside, unbeknownst to happy relatives, clear as a bell to Yuri Sen, lying tongueless in the bed beside.

Mice, said Yuri Sen, can smell a partner's genes, and will not mate if they are too closely related, I was almost afraid it would come to that, that I would wake one day and find myself attuned not only to the substance of each person, but also to their histories, that one day I might be able to olfactorise their destinies, smell each individual fate.

One morning he woke to the fetor of an old man in the bed beside him, dying slowly of some lingering disease, a ring of men around him, all smelling of hair oil and lime soap and betelnut juice. There was one who carried about him the smell of the droppings of a recently strangled parrot, he wore, as Yuri Sen was able to see when he came into view, a cream-coloured Nehru suit, and rarely left his post beside the old man, though his eyes, his keen eyes, seemed always upon him, Yuri Sen, manacled by his own muscles to his bed, his eyes were always upon him, as were the eyes of the other men and women who came and went, ostensibly to visit the old man, but in reality, Yuri Sen was convinced after a few days, to see him.

Why, why, he wondered, am I such a curiosity, or perhaps this is some complex delusion scored upon his reason by the sharp slivers of the continuously proliferating odours, a feeble fantasy of a mind ravaged by the mad march of smells, dividing and multiplying, like the sheep that he had forgotten to count every time he had courted sleep in that tedious and trusty fashion, still lined up expectantly in the recesses of his subconscious, am I imagining this vigilance, he wondered, or is this old man truly a front, can it be that they are all watching *me*?

I visit him in the evenings, read him the newspapers, and occasionally some poetry. He closes his eyes and listens, forced like a sponge to absorb all that flows towards him from my lips, I spare him nothing, drench his living corpse in the emotional history of Bengal, I read to him from Bibhuti Banerji's epic novel, which absorbs me to such an extent that I begin to hope he will not wake until I have reached the end, and indeed a day arrives when I am at the last page, and he is staring mute at my moving lips as I read, *On such peaceful evenings he has sat by the banks of the Ichhamoti under piled bloodclouds, and contemplated the immensity of the universe. As a child, he would fish beneath the thorny trees and dream of lands he had never seen – now his consciousness soars beyond the tight compass of his childhood fantasies evermore on the wings of light towards the great skies – often he finds comfort in the thought that this universe is neither humble nor mean, that its currency is the light year, that its darkness is studded with galaxies and solar systems, the invisible ether expands beyond the confines of the human imagination, into such a universe has he been born . . .*

I can detect an impatience in Yuri Sen's dark eyes, how can this quest end? he wonders, he has traced with me the fortunes of the protagonist, who has come in these final pages to leave his son at his village, before he travels abroad to Fiji and Samoa. He has returned after twenty-four years to his village, his childhood, with his son, the son who has never seen so many birds as now, never known the names of so many flowers and herbs, the child steps into the ruin of his grandfather's house, the yard is overgrown, strewn with bricks and bamboo sticks, are there no birds here?

A sudden wind lifts in welcome towards the young boy, and with it come the ghosts of his ancestors, the lame Biru Ray, his grandfather Harihar Ray, his grandmother Sarbajoya, his aunt Durga, dead of pneumonia many years ago, many years ago his father had discovered a necklace that she had been suspected of stealing, concealed his dead sister's misdeed in the thick of pondslime, her ghost stretches her arms out now to his son, twenty-four years later, there you are, welcome home, his ancestors cry, welcome home.

And beyond this. From the shadows emerge myths, there under his grandmother's tree lies Vishma on his bed of arrows, under the bushes the warrior Karna, there is Arjun with his fearful bow, the hapless Vanumati, the charioted Krishna, and the vanquished king Duryadhan, the tearful Janoki. Wandering the heat-hazed fields is the destitute cowherd Trijat, who welcomes him, welcomes him, there you are, do you not know us, so many afternoons you have sat at the broken window face to face with us, do come . . . please . . . do come . . .

Come out of there, you naughty boy, a voice calls to him, and halts, seeing him there among the bushes, the very image of his father.

Such is the mystery of life that unvanquished it resurfaces in all its glory, time and time again, this eternal cycle of the universe.

After twenty-four years, the prodigal son has returned home.

I shut the book, and stare for a while, overcome with emotion, at the linoleum floor. Yuri Sen has closed his eyes, I take my handkerchief and gently wipe away the small tears that have gathered like beads of glass in the creases of his lower lids. Suddenly I am prodded by a man in a cream-coloured Nehru suit who has been sitting all this while by the side of a neighbouring patient, you are disturbing him, he accuses me, you are distracting him.

That is for me to decide, I tell him firmly.

You must not disturb him, the man repeats.

I would be obliged if you would mind your own business, I say.

He shakes his head, you do not understand, he says, we will not let you disturb him.

I see, I reply and stalk out, I demand to see the Ward Superintendent, but he is of little use, what can we do? he asks me.

Move the patient, I suggest.

I will see what I can do, he says.

Out of the corner of his eye Yuri Sen saw him extract a phial from a pocket of his cream-coloured Nehru suit, he is going to kill me, he thought, he will poison me before I am polluted by poetry and remain a mere mortal when my breath returns, if it returns, my breath, my poor breath.

But the man only touches the bottle to his forehead, unscrews the top and sprinkles the contents over the length of Yuri Sen's useless body, a trail of drops leads from his chest down to his swollen toes, holy water from the Ganges, Yuri Sen can smell its crystalline origins, fetters of ice shrinking together, the slow parturitions of the glacial mass pulse in his mind, the clean cold birth of a great river sears his senses, the droplets collect at the base of his tongue, conglobe, tremble, and shoot out ten thousand branches around his solid bones, and wither all but one which gathers force and streams sugary with the sap of Himalayan cedars towards the plains, Yuri Sen can smell the first trembling descent into the dry wheatfields, the bleached white ribcage of the earth struggling to contain the growing force of the waters, the river widens and accumulates the miseries of its people, swells with the odours of cholera and kala-azar, rotting fish, cheap toothpaste, dead flowers, old promises, flourpaste glue, examination booklets, cigarette foils, cracked dentures, clarified butter, lost digits, used syringes, broken idols, stale cardamom, tax returns, discarded batteries, dry white seasons, grain alcohol, strangled parrots, bruised coriander, broken sitar strings, shrivelled land deeds, moribund ploughs, hookworm larvae, hardnosed bargains, kerosene lamps, missing mangoes, trigonometry texts, unused watercolours, unremarkable sunsets, adulterated sugar, unburnt oil, Yuri Sen smells gratefully among all this the tender flanks of a newly drowned calf, the fragrant musings of a village girl on the eve of her wedding, the ripening bouquet of retting jute, as the river carves a steady course from disaster through disease finally to decay, the mouth frozen with siltsores, Yuri Sen can smell the bubbling mud, the dissolving fibres of blood, milk and tears, the wide scream of the river as it meets the sea.

He remembers how he and his cousins had once encountered a pair of lovers on a bench beside the river, it was the summer after his O-levels, his parents had sent him to Calcutta to recover, a boisterous uncle had decided to take his nephews and nieces for a spin in his new jeep, parked it by the river and taken them on a night-time stroll by the Ganges, and there they had bumped into the lovers, clasped together upon the creaky bench, huddled together in a mysterious paroxysm of unfulfilled desire, the intensity of their lust had startled him, while his cousins giggled mercilessly, Yuri Sen had caught his breath, and experienced a strange envy, his uncle had urged them to move on, although before they were out of earshot to tease them he had burst into song, *how can I hold back this night that passes, tears flow from my eyes, take these clothes, this garland of flowers has become unbearable, that such a night should pass without you*, the children began to laugh, their uncle lowered himself onto a stone step, and sang in suddenly serious tones, *I have come to these shores on a futile quest, overburdened with dreams and hopes, I will return emptyhanded, as always*, the children puzzled by this abrupt change in their uncle's mood shifted uneasily by the moonlit river, slapping mosquitoes on their bare arms and calves. Yuri Sen stood staring at the turbid waters, still recovering from the onslaught of the couple's desperate lust, *once and for all, spring is over in my life*, their uncle sang, and then with a bright sigh, turned to them and said in English, what do you say to some Chinese food, kids.

Where are they now? he wonders, my cousins, my uncles and aunts, how little they know of my predicament, for them I have simply vanished into the alienating embrace of the West, if only they knew how near I was, if they knew of my condition, would they not rush to my bedside, take over the duties and the expenses, or would they? His uncles are old now, his cousins might be quite indifferent to his fate, busy as they must be with their own lives. He remembers the last time he visited the old Broad Street house, he had come to say goodbye, for his studies in Shantiniketan were finished, he was going home, with Fiona, he brought her with him to introduce to his cousins, pale Fiona, still weak from a recent attack of paratyphoid, how he enjoyed nursing her, holding cold compresses to her forehead, feeding her watery fish stew, fanning her during the many power failures, while she slept he would gaze upon her soft sunburnt features and muse that he had reached the limits of happiness, his existence was complete, he had looked over the line of her shoulders and seen that his life had nowhere further to go.

Where are you staying? his uncles had asked reproachfully.

At the Fairlawn, he had replied stiffly.

Why not with us, an aunt demanded tartly.

Fiona hasn't been well, he mumbled, she needs rest.

We would have made her comfortable, they insisted.

We didn't want to trouble you, said Yuri Sen.

That afternoon, while Fiona rested in heavy curtained bliss, Yuri Sen walked into the trembling heat to roam for the last time the streets of the city that he had not been able to make his home. Three years before, he had given up a place at Cambridge to return to this land, I want to be a Bengali, he had proudly declared to his flabbergasted parents. You think you can become a Bengali just like that? his father had taunted, just by immersing yourself in the culture after so many years?

You are Bengali, his mother had insisted, your blood is ours, you speak the language, we have even made sure that all of you can read and write it, how much more Bengali can you be?

If I can truly speak and read and write Bengali, how is it that I don't understand a word of the Tagore dance drama I am in, retorted Yuri Sen, how is it that I have to have every syllable of *Chitrangada* explained to me. My God, if this part weren't without words, it would never have been offered to me!

Even I have problems understanding Tagore, his father said,

you can't worry about not understanding Bengali poetry.

That is precisely what I do worry about, said Yuri Sen.

Esha's mother offered flowers from her shrine to take to him, Yuri Sen, still beyond our reason, trapped within his own horizons, Yuri Sen, times on times he divided and measured space by space in his ninefold darkness, death was not, but eternal life sprung, somewhere within the metal of his thoughts, his prolific despair obscured more and more, in dark secrecy hiding in surging sulphurous fluid his fantasies, his memories, scooping and dividing time, numbering the links on the chain to hours, days, years.

He is in a holy trance, the man in the cream-coloured suit insists, lighting incense under his bed, sprinkling his sheets with holy water, burying Yuri Sen under a deluge of smells, to be divided and measured and classified before he could dismiss them, the barrage of multiplying smells.

This is no holy trance, I tell the man and his saffron-suited minions, he is suffering from acute post-infection polyneuropathy, please leave him alone, I beg them.

He is no saint, I tell them, he is no prophet, Yuri Sen.

And one day he wakes to a strange hammering in his head, the dull echo tripping down his inert backbone like the unfortunate perambulator on the Odessa steps. His ribs bend cavernous towards the overture of his flesh, the new pangs of hope, a craving hunger rises through his channelled throat, his tongue burns fearfully, he is come to life, we exclaim, as the doctor injects morphine, and orders the tubes to be gradually removed.

For a week he lies in deathly dream, twitching and moaning, delivered from nerveless silence into raw dismal pain, all smells congeal once more into a grey mass, all words are divested of their glass sheaths and now dig their heels once more into his brain, uninsulated, naked, he is in a state of protracted birth, he struggles like a blue newborn for his first breath, by degrees achieves his equilibrium with the surrounding gases, is whole again, but weak, and in delirium. We sit by his side quietly now, waiting for him to recover his senses, waiting as he reforges his uncreated conscience, waiting as he reconstitutes his nerves and muscles, so that he might wake again into this world.

When he finally comes to his senses, they are waiting, the man in the cream-coloured Nehru suit, his saffron-robed followers. All night they have kept vigil, now as the dawn shakes like a wet crow wing through the slatted clouds, they hear him stir, and light a holy taper, so that fire might be witness to his rising, they sprinkle holy water upon the clammy bedclothes that mould to the shape of his long and wasted form, so that he resembles all the more a mummified ascetic, they rub turmeric up the palms of his still unfeeling soles.

He wakes to the calls of the first morning vendors, hawking young coconuts for weary mothers who have sat all night beside their sick children, men and women who have tended their dying parents, their ill husbands and wives, he wakes to the sounds of the night nurses preparing to leave their posts and return to their lonely rooms to sleep, he wakes to clink of boiled eggs for breakfast, the soft thud of bananas upon each food tray, he wakes to a motorcycle engine revving outside his window as the uncle of a child prepares to take the news of its death to the grandparents, he wakes to the smells of disinfectant and incense. The man in the cream-coloured suit, freshly groomed, presses his large hands together and implores him, please speak, give us your blessings, we have been waiting for your blessings.

They come now into focus, the hopeful men, fresh *tilaks* painted on their foreheads, give us your blessing, their leader pleads.

He closes his eyes, his world teems with vast enormities, frightening, faithless, fawning, where his new thoughts crouch beside his old, still only touching fingers, he remembers on the last evening of their life together, he and Fiona had taken a picnic supper out to Hampstead Heath, they had spent the day painting the flat they had just bought in Dartmouth Park, the kitchen was now a delightful eggshell yellow, the spare bedroom/nursery an acceptable blue. They sat in their overalls eating chicken salad sandwiches by the Heath ponds, the sky darkened, and they were alone, except for the bobbing lights of two hopeful anglers and their dogs. Can these be the limits of my life, he had wondered, touching a cool paintflecked palm, I have never been so happy, he had told Fiona, I have never felt so calm.

Give us your blessings, the men implore, give us your blessings.

Do you know, asks Yuri Sen, how mice steal eggs?

St Valentine's Day, 1994, Robin Underhill draws the curtains to find the spires dressed in a thin coating of snow. The grass bristles through the sparse blanket of white giving the grounds a strange unshaven look, minor flurries still float delicately past. He longs for the snowstorm to last, so that he may live in sublime excommunication, at least for a while. All night the winds have howled, all night he has held the past in his mouth like an unboiled egg, and yet managed profitably to write, the final chapter of his book is now complete but for a few references, the sky is grey, it may snow again, he has not bought a Valentine's gift for his wife, tonight they will dine out somewhere, where? She will have made plans, he has students arriving in half an hour, after that he should go home and rest, for he has only had an hour's sleep all night, and in that hour dreamt that he has made his peace with you, that you have met him under the stiff arches of your past, clad in brown tweeds, and smiling held out your hands, that he has taken joyfully and covered with friendly kisses. Alexandra Vorobyova, where are you now? he wonders, into what inferno have you descended in the wake of that trickster, the perfidious puppetmaker, Juan Gorrion, the last time he had seen him, almost thirty years ago, he had been standing outside the college lodge gobbling candied hearts, thirty years ago, a bagful of little hearts that a woman friend had given him in protest against his conduct towards the fairer sex, have some, Gorrion had said, thrusting the bag under Robin Underhill's nose, have some they're delicious, he had picked one out and held it between thumb and forefinger, I could put one inside each puppet, he had said laughing, do you think they would last, Robin?

At least as long as your puppets, Robin Underhill had replied, feeling awkward and unimaginative.

I could construct a whole viscera out of confectionary, Gorrion had mused in delight, he had thrown a handful of hearts at an approaching friend, welcome to the puppeteer's breakfast, he had called. This curious expression, long forgotten by its author, had lodged itself in Underhill's mind, teasing him incessantly, as if its meaning lurked somewhere behind a corner, the puppeteer's breakfast, and the ghost of Gorrion laughs, not quite at him, but not with him, either, the ghost of Gorrion, what is there to say that he is not truly a ghost, now, what is to say that he has not been consumed by the flames that he has walked into, dragging you with him. But no, Robin Underhill is sure, whatever might happen to you, Gorrion is sure to escape as always unscathed.

Trust you to fall into his trap, Juan Gorrion. The only woman I will ever love is my cousin Sophia, he had told Robin Underhill, once, after a night of heavy drinking, their friends scattered in various states of sleep about Gorrion's study, Robin Underhill struggling himself to stay awake, Gorrion fresh as a daisy, lighting one cigar after the other. The only woman I will ever love is Sophia, he had said slowly, but she has gone and married some American reporter, a liquorice bitterness rose in his voice, she is a housewife, now, in Omaha, Nebraska. Can you believe it, asked Juan Gorrion, his consonants softening, she is a bloody housewife in Omaha, Nebraska.

Robin Underhill had wondered within his alcoholic haze whether he would ever experience such extremes of passion, or was he forever doomed to woo simply with wit and wise affection. Juan Gorrion's gaze floated above the cigar smoke like a sheen of olive oil, I dream of her every night, he said, I will dream of her every night until I die.

It was the theatricality of his every action, no doubt untempered by age, that must have drawn him to you, blindly you had followed him into the depths of his own disaster, to which he was immune, but you were not. Did you not know this, looking into his eyes, the rainbow colours of an old oil expanding within a dark puddle that it longs to escape.

Tell me, Gorrion had asked you, in the throes of passion, tell me why you left him, your husband, what happened, tell me?

And you had never given him a name, Robin Underhill, you had not given Gorrion the opportunity to exclaim, and seizing you by your bare shoulders say, but I knew him, I knew him at college, you married *him*, Robin Underhill?

You had never given him a name, oh he was just plain colourless, you had said, knowing that this, when it appeared in print, as all of Gorrion's experiences one way or the other came to do, would crack like glass inside him, Robin Underhill, even though it was he who had left you, I need a certain peace, he had told you, I need a certain peace that you will never be able to give me.

Peace that now curls and knots within him like thin stone, Robin Underhill blinks at the bright snow. Did you ever find him, he wonders, find him buried deep in dull alcohol in some seedy hotel room under a naked bulb, reading Cyrillic horoscopes and drinking cheap kvass, why have you followed me, Gorrion would ask, can you not respect the limits of lust?

And you would have faced him, your hair aflame in the dying sunlight and the sudden flares of torpedoes, and grinding the gunsmoke settled thick upon your lips, you would have replied, what do you know of the limits of lust?

You should not have followed me, he would answer, plucking his words as if with the bow of a lacerated violin, you should not have followed me, only one woman ever had the right to follow me, and she gave it up to boil beef and bake pecan pies in Omaha, Nebraska.

And you would have turned away from him, your hair a live prison of vicious gold, your waist churned out of the twilight like an hourglass of ash, you would reply, what would you know of the baking of pecan pies?

But in the morning he would be gone, only a thin shadow of gunpowder in your arms, leaving you with no leads and fewer secrets, only the address of a mental hospital where they kept shellshocked children, where you would go and wait, and tend to the crazed children, bathe their pimpled foreheads, run combs through their tangled hair, teach them Russian rhymes, until the day would come when you would all have to flee, thinks Robin Underhill, staring into the unvarnished snow and cursing the paucity of his imagination.

You would meet him once again, for the last time, between a crack in two mountains, hardly wide enough for the both of you, this ravenous lust, he would complain, this inexplicable lust that keeps bringing us together, he would complain, swallowing your mouth in his own lying lips, why do you keep following me? he would ask, with mock tenderness, his fingers bruising your thighs. Only one woman in the world ever had the right to follow me, and she gave it up to mince radish and make marmalade, he would have said, thumbing the mossy clefts left by months of dull cold, months of ice water snatched from tin buckets, and damp-flannelled heat trickling like suet into the groin. Why do you so scorn my quest? you would ask him, why do you so misprise this undertaking, my search for you?

Because it lacks true dedication, he would reply, it is no more than a foxhunt, a purple pigsticking, a grand perversion, you stalk me like a clown in search of the carnival, but how can an eagle know what is in the pit, any more than the mole?

You speak in riddles, Juan Gorrion.

Does an eagle know what is in the pit? he will ask you, ramming you against the wall of stone as the gap starts to close, can wisdom be put in a silver rod, he whispers, thrusting deep into you, can wisdom be put in a silver rod, or love in a golden bowl? he asks as the stone starts to close over you, he crouches between your thighs, and before the rock can crush you both, he has slipped out through a thin crevice, Juan Gorrion, quick as a sparrow, here today Gorrion tomorrow, Chuck Chattington had said of him, Robin Underhill remembers, for Chuck had taken Juan Gorrion to his parents for his first Christmas, all the way to Greenwich, Connecticut, his parents had sent tickets for both him and his foreign friend, a simple act of Christian charity, Charles Chattington Sr had explained to his surprised son, Chuck had lost his passport on the plane and had been detained at immigration while Gorrion waited smugly outside with his parents, but although he was charming to them, their wholesome company had not suited him, he had left rather suddenly on Boxing Day with Chuck's older brother for Manhattan where he'd had a hell of a time, he told the peeved Chuck later when they were back in Oxford (they had not even flown back together for Gorrion had managed to extend his visit a few extra days so that he could attend the première of one of Chuck's brother's friend's girlfriend's experimental films), here today, Gorrion tomorrow, Chuck had said regretfully to Robin Underhill, quite a character, this man Gorrion.

Yet you had not seen through him, not even as your ribs were crushed to ice by infolding rock, mortarstruck, you had not considered his faithlessness, even when he slipped between your wet thighs and crawled out through the crowding gap of rock into stormlight, the aching wilderness and the thunder of war.

You only felt your breath rise as plucked from bruised violin strings, felt yourself made finally whole by the strength of rock against your fragmented identities, and offered your last gasp as a prayer for each daughter bought and each son sold, your last breath, that Robin Underhill had once hoped he might curl about his palm, and take with him, in his aged grief, to some riverside bench, and smooth between his gnarled fingers, only to fold back again into a knotted fist, how I wanted to grow old with you, Alexandra Vorobyova, sighs Robin Underhill, staring out into the melting snow, how I wish we had made our peace, many years ago, when the world was still yellow, and the footprints of man were still fresh on the moon.

He has pushed away all thoughts of his daughter for a while now, ever since he left her, small and worn, clutching her polythene bag of cake and cheese, and the sheaf of pound notes he had stuffed into her hand. I can only survive by blocking out that whole section of my past, he had reasoned between tormented fits of sleep in the nights that followed, I can only go on by blocking out that whole segment of my history, he had told himself, between shards of Wagner, the overture to *Tannhäuser* that his wife insisted on playing with her bedtime stretching exercises, every night.

But this snow now, strangely decorative, reduces these arches to the gingerbread texture of lesser breeds, bringing to mind that North American winter, the dropsical portico where he had met you, your fiery locks tumbling out from under your green shawl, your hands small and white under sinister green gloves. You must be the Englishman, you had said to him, blowing on your naked fingers, as if keeping alive some hidden flame, you must be the Englishman, you had said, in an accent so delicious he felt like cramming his mouth with snow, my gloves are wet, you explained, blowing hard upon your porcelain fingers, take mine, said Robin Underhill, I have another pair in my car.

Then I will take the pair in your car, you had said very seriously.

Take these, he had implored, I am not cold, really I am not.

The others had arrived before they could settle the matter, they trooped through the crisp snow to the parking lot where his rented steed slumbered. You had retrieved a pair of woollen mitts from the glove compartment, and also set loose a shower of photographs, all of Eleanor, his fiancée, he had explained rather awkwardly, Eleanor, who had graciously received him once again when his tryst with you had expired, Eleanor, mother of his sons, Eleanor who exercised to Wagner, every night and every morn, and served him parsnips on Sundays, simply swimming in butter.

Take me to the sea, said Yuri Sen, take me to the sea, so that I might breathe in triplicate, now that I can breathe again.

We booked a cottage in a new holiday resort in Puri, and took him down by train, arranging him on the top tier so that he could sleep undisturbed throughout the journey, although the heat was fierce enough already to toss him and turn him all night like an omelette restless in its pan. The child hardly slept either, whining all night for milk. We were delivered by the Jagannath Express, a sorry bunch, but for Esha's mother, who had slept soundly all through, and brighteyed found us some breakfast, organised rickshaws to take us to our holiday village.

I hoisted Yuri Sen onto the seat, and climbed in beside him, put my bag across his knees to secure him in this position, but held onto him anyway as we rode gently beneath the noonday sun towards the sea, teasing glimpses of angry blue through the casuarina trees that many years ago had caused Esha to gasp in delight when we came here for our honeymoon, her father had booked us into the Railway Lodge, whose colonial sumptuousness had overwhelmed me to the point where it had almost struck a chord of misery within Esha, to see me wallow in sherry trifles and starched sheets, to find my mind so occupied by the pursuit of comfort instead of our connubial bliss. She would catch herself wondering, while we made love, what part of my pleasure was in the comfort of lush pillow and what part in the tender fulfilment of our long-dammed passion. It will pass, she would tell herself, it will pass, she would reassure herself, as she filed her nails and steeled herself for the life we would return to in Calcutta, in our cramped flat, cooking for seven adults and one child over two spluttery gas rings, hunting out corners to hang out wet clothes in times of rain, enduring the steady stream of relatives come from distant corners of the city to wish us well, to inspect the new bride. Sometimes she would escape to the quiet of her parents' home, to work on her thesis, she would tell my parents, who were understanding enough, never objected to these occasional retreats, not to her face, at least. All this was yet to come, and she saw it ahead not with apprehension, but rather with the terrified calm of a dedicated mountaineer, she gritted her teeth against her new future and coated her nails with clear polish, while I lay beside her struggling with H. G. Wells's *Kipps*, which she insisted I read, but the sweet afternoon heat made the words stick and roll into each other, my English is not good enough, I told her, slamming the small book shut. She looked disappointed, perhaps you can read it to me, I consoled her, playfully snatching her bottle of nailpolish. Give that back, she said, smiling. Why do you paint your nails in invisible colours, I asked. Would you rather I painted them a bright red? she teased. Whatever you like, I replied, burying my face in a cool expanse of pillow. Outside the sea roared graciously, it would be the last time she painted her nails, cooking for seven people every night turned the polish a scabby yellow, she was better off with unvarnished nails, my mother complained that she dressed too plainly, her younger son's wife, bright and talented she might be, my mother would complain to her sisters, bright and talented, but not a beauty.

She has grace, her sisters would console, a rare dignity that shines through the darkness of her skin.

She is so thin though, my mother would say, she never eats

enough, and she is always rushing around, I wish she would give up her job.

Her job paid for your new glasses, my brother's wife would remind her quietly.

So it did, my mother would reply, I should not complain, she is a good girl, she is always doing her best to make us happy. But I cannot shake off the feeling that she is cursed, her every light sandalstep seems to drag with it the echo of a strange doom, I do not know what it is, said my mother, but it chills me.

After her first miscarriage, we came again to Puri to recover our spirits, this time to a small roach-infested hotel where we would wake every morning to strains of Orissi pop music, the sun beating through the thin curtains, shake yesterday's sand out of our shoes and stumble down to the beach for a breakfast of fresh *rasgollas*, spend the morning reading on the beach until the fierce sun drove us back to our hotel, where after a large and insipid lunch we would sleep late into the afternoon, return to the beach to watch the waters darken. Cheated of sunset, the waves would froth into oblivion, and spreading ourselves upon the warm sand, we would talk, raise our eyes to the incredible heavens, if there are any great truths out there, she had said, I pray that they might be revealed to you, she had said suddenly once, drunk with the thunder of the restless ocean. She had desired my greatness with a passion that frightened me, if there are any great truths out there, I had replied, gesturing to the stars, I would rather they remained hidden.

When she was a little stronger, we made the customary day trip to Konarak, the chariot temple, it rested upon its decaying wheels with a stubborn timelessness that penetrated my soul like the dull shriek of a great brass gong, I scrutinised the eroding erotic friezes with a fierce detachment, those very same carvings whose explicit nature had so embarrassed me a few years ago on our honeymoon, I examined them now with emotion, and felt for the first time since our marriage, a profound bitterness, what had we achieved, we had tried to have a child and failed, I was teaching in a small college, she in a miserable school, where could life take us, I felt a strange distaste for our existence, face to face with the red sandstone upon which the erotic ecstasies of our ancestors had been so coldly inscribed, I cursed the smallness of my fate. A lizard gathered upon a curved stone thigh, I watched Esha come towards me, we had agreed to circle the temple in different directions but I had barely moved, she halted by my side, I once had a dream, she said, that you and I were stranded penniless in a foreign country, in some post-apocalyptic, but also hugely ancient time, like being transported suddenly to Babylon perhaps, and we had to struggle to make ends meet, I dreamt that one evening you returned with a gift for me, a shawl, or a sari, I cannot remember which, held it up smiling for me to see, that was my dream, said Esha. I clutched her hand and slowly lifted myself back onto the plane of our happiness, it was the first time that I had slipped, in the years to come it would happen again, but less and less often, by the time we moved to her parents' house, I had attained a state of perfect equilibrium. I believe we might have stayed there forever, poised perfectly between light and shade, pain and laughter, and a hundred other dualities, we may have stayed forever in this supreme balance of the senses, if one morning I had not woken up and discovered how to turn gold into grass.

They must have left over a year ago, she tells him, the young woman in tartan leggings, we moved in towards the end of summer, she says, have you come a long way? she asks Robin Underhill.

Only from Oxford, he replies.

I have a whole pile of things, she says, that must have belonged to them, you can look through them if you want, though I suppose I oughtn't to give them to you, I keep meaning to take them over to the letting agency, but I suppose they'd only throw them away, nothing precious in there, just odds and ends . . .

She returns with a Marks & Spencer's shopping bag, not a lot here really of any worth, she says, you might as well take it, just leave me an address or something in case someone ever comes hunting for things.

I can always return them to you, he offers.

Don't bother, she says, I'm glad to get rid of them.

He leaves the woman his college address, and clutching the bag almost with awe he descends, Robin Underhill, his head feels light with exhaustion, he has driven all morning on three cups of coffee and nothing else through ghastly blizzard and frightful traffic, for at dawn a sudden pain had stabbed through his sleep like a saint's calling, and he had lifted his head off the pile of page proofs, knowing that the time had come to find her again, his daughter, child that he had abandoned once to the mercies of a restless mother, and later abandoned again herself to monstrous motherhood. The time had come to find her, and this time to lodge her securely within the arc of his own life, that her ghost might cease to divide his dreams into stark repetitive instalments, and beggar the opera of his conscience to a few raw strings. Last week, a black-edged card had arrived, announcing your father's funeral, it had given him a brief sense of hope, perhaps it was Anya who had sent it, perhaps she had returned to the quiet fold of her grandparents, given her child away, and returned to civilisation, to peace, to hot chocolate and peppermint schnapps, and the agony of midterm exams, the narrow college beds creaking under impatient desires, this was the life he had imagined for her ten years ago, watching her suck biscuits, sitting across from him in her grandparents' living room, he had seen her future then in the lighter shades of snow, in the smaller shade of sorrel and sassafras, he had seen her life unfold, and he had seen himself within it as the slender thread of blood that leads the calf out of the abattoir, as a mess of pigeons' footprints in the corner of the screen, so be it, he had said to himself, and returned to his new family in North Oxford.

But the time has come now to remember beyond the games

that he had played with her as an infant, the maps and botanical engravings he would hold open for her small eyes to feast upon, the guinea pigs in the pet shop that she so wanted, that you would not let her have, the time has come now to cast his mind back beyond the daffodils that they had picked together for you, daffodils that you had thrust in salt instead of water, and served fried in batter to his astonished friends. If you are wondering where the daffodils are, he had told the bewildered child the following morning, your mother fried them for supper, he had said, spooning egg into her reluctant mouth, your bloody mother served my colleagues fried daffodils.

The throbbing bundle beneath his arm, Robin Underhill stumbles into the Lolita Steak House and orders a chicken liver kebab, seats himself at a redtopped table and lays his loot upon the scratched Formica. Lolita Steak House, he muses, fire of my sirloin, he chuckles quietly, McAllister will enjoy that one, says Robin Underhill to himself. He shakes out gently the contents of the Marks & Spencer's shopping bag. There is a sketchpad, obviously Anya's, filled with several likenesses of Yuri Sen, there is a bottle of clear nail varnish, a slim Bengali novel on the back of which has been hastily scrawled $(1-x(1-x)/x)^x = e^{-x(1-x)}$, there is an inflatable neck pillow, a small jade rabbit missing an ear, a mintsized Dutch tile, a jar of cucumber foot cream, a crumpled batik silk tie, a box of stock cubes, and a postcard of the Queen Mother, never sent, saying upon it in your hand, A big THANK YOU for all your help, love, Alexandra, PS. Hope the cactus has survived. Robin Underhill inspects it carefully, once he has recovered from the shock of your handwriting, so alive, there, suddenly, beneath his fingertips, there is an address, and it is addressed to 'Rose' but no surname, perhaps that was why you had waited to send it, you could not remember her surname, the address is a council flat close to Paddington, hardly five minutes' walk from the Lolita Steak House. Robin Underhill bites into his chicken liver kebab, and with the first assault of pickled pepper upon his senses, decides that he will deliver the postcard, years later as it may be, and perhaps if he is lucky this will lead on to some other tantalising clue . . . wiping his lips with his napkin, Robin Underhill feels a curious thrill, a schoolboyish excitement to which he knows he must not succumb, lest his search for his daughter be reduced to a picture puzzle that in piecing together he might lose sight of the whole. So many times in his academic excursions has one chase led to another and distracted him from his original purpose, that now he hardly dares define a scheme, leaves his sleuthing sensibilities to wander at will through the jungles of ethnobotanical fact, at the end of it all there is always a book, not one that he had set out to write, but some other entirely, begging a title, begging a theme, he examines the cheap postcard in his hands, he knows that to find his daughter he must not be overwhelmed by the scent of the hunt.

He pays at the counter for his kebab and wanders out into the afternoon murk, the skies are heavy with the promise of rain, he consults his London A to Z for the shortest route to his destination, arrives soaked to the skin, the stairs are strewn like church steps with rice, and bits of grass, perhaps he should risk the lift, but before he can make up his mind, an ambulance pulls up at the entrance screeching wildly, two ambulance workers pass by him with a stretcher, Robin Underhill loses his nerve, if he were to knock on her door, and find her dead, the mysterious 'Rose', or what if he were to barge in upon a circle of drug addicts preparing their afternoon fix, 'Rose' could well be a Gothic punk, or an anorexic waif, he had assumed she was an old woman, but who could tell, Robin Underhill rushes hurriedly back into the rain, sprints back to Paddington where a train is waiting, poised to leave as he hops on board, to take him back to Oxford.

He runs his fingers through his wet hair, and blows hard upon knuckles to swamp the chill of this unfinished episode, 'Rose', another ghost to swell his dreams, another phantom at the puppeteer's breakfast, 'Rose', who might she have been, some old lover of Gorrion's perhaps, was it her number he had left you under the toothglass, perhaps it was 'Rose' who had furnished his trail for you, 'Rose', the mysterious cactus lady, murdered this afternoon by fellow spies. Underhill, your mind is wandering, he tells himself, and digging into the Marks & Spencer's bag he pulls out the sketchpad, seeking sanity in his daughter's drawings, her rough pen and ink portraits of Yuri Sen, of you, of me, of Sir Percival playing the flute, and then a few clean pages, and one of me again, languishing upon the sofa, a fat book balanced on my forehead. In one of his lighter moments, tiptoeing past the boundaries of his humour, and already dreading the consequences, he had given the sketch a name, 'Promothesh bound' he had dubbed it, Yuri Sen.

He sits at a card table, drinking in the sea air and fiddling with the cuffs of his dark green shirt, too loose upon his emaciated frame. I would be grateful for a game of chess, he says to me, lighting a cigarette, will you play chess with me? asks Yuri Sen.

Only in jest, I answer.

Never in jest, says he.

What are the stakes, I ask.

If you win, says Yuri Sen, I will finish your autobiography.

Rather, if you win, I reply, will I suffer you to finish my autobiography.

As you like, says Yuri Sen.

Robin Underhill turns the page and confronts a strange set of interlaced hieroglyphs, your fluid plans to reconstruct my life, to wrap my terrible journey towards truth in salad leaves and coleslaw, to thresh my ambitions from the stars, so that hundreds of hands might paw my dreams, you had hoped to weave the threadbare events of my past into a system of helices to encoil those prurient readers who would buy my experiences for little more than the price of a song.

He flicks a stray spider off his frayed cuff, it lands upon the chessboard, Yuri Sen lights another cigarette, it was a good game, he concedes.

I pack the pieces away into the ivory box, squash the spider with the King pawn, and wipe up the mess with my handkerchief.

That was unnecessary, says Yuri Sen.

What was?

Killing the spider, he says, drawing hard upon his cigarette.

I suppose so, I reply.

Take me to the shore, says Yuri Sen.

That may be difficult, I tell him. For we had been fooled in Calcutta into booking rooms in a holiday village miles from the sea, the private beach is accessible only through a forest reserve. I inquire at reception whether there is a vehicle to take us there, give us half an hour, they tell me, anxious not to disappoint the invalid, their guilt at conning us doubled by the sight of his wasted limbs, his withered form, Yuri Sen, dreadful in convalescence, like a malnourished Adonis, his countenance a cabinet of asymmetries, fearful to behold.

I was born in winter, reads Robin Underhill, I was born to a chill dawn, and the calls of shivering vultures, gathered around an oily puddle outside my mother's window. The nurse held me over a hotplate, he may live yet, she said to my mother, I was two months premature, my eyes moved under my lids like marbles in jelly, my head barely filled the inside of a teacup, my fingers guarded passionately the wrinkles upon my palms, my dubious destiny hung upon a glass thread that trembled dangerously under the heavyfeathered breathing of the nurse, as she turned me from side to side over the hotplate, until my substance took on the colours of flesh, my jaw stirred, my eyes began to swim under their pale lids, he is beautifully formed, declared the nurse.

They leave us upon the beach with a young boy who sets up an umbrella for Yuri Sen to recline beneath, and promises to guide me through the treacherous waves if I should want to swim. We send him back to the hotel for a flask of cool yoghurt, he sets off disappointed tying his towel around his head to protect himself from the fierce afternoon sun. The sea spars with the sky in flashes of scrubbed white and steel, the waves rise in sore-throated agony and crumble like ash upon the shore, this is awful, says Yuri Sen.

It was your idea, I remind him.

It was my idea, he agrees.

He pulls out from his cloth satchel a pad of ruled paper, shall we start at the beginning? asks Yuri Sen.

I did not learn to speak until I was almost three years old, reads Robin Underhill, they thought I might never speak, that life had been held out to me on too narrow a ledge for all my faculties to flourish. It was clear I was not stupid for I would fit together jigsaw puzzles with alarming speed, those that my brother left lying around, and his broken toys I would put together, long before I could speak.

Whose life could this be, wonders Robin Underhill, that you have dared take on in the first person, what sorry genius cowered behind the colourless almanac, whose life had you violated thus, whose poor history had you taken this time in vain to call your own?

The boy returns with our yoghurt, and asks our permission to go for a swim, he strips down to his underwear, ties his thin towel around his waist and runs over the burning sand towards the sea. Yuri Sen stops scribbling, distracted by the boy's figure, darting like a twig from crest to crest, let me see what you have written, I ask, extracting the notebook from his hands.

My first experience of life was the warmth of the anvil, I read of my own life, for I had been expelled unforged from the womb, the nurse placed me upon a hotplate hoping to draw some life out of my cryptic lungs, she turned me from this side to that, easing heat into my stonecoiled bowels. Later watching my wife make chapattis upon the gas ring, I would always remember how my life had begun with much the same movements, that life had broadened within me much as the gases swelled the cheeks of flatbread, the warmth from the hotplate had spread through the miniature mazes of my capillaries, warm threads of heat had coursed through the frail architecture of my liver, emboldened my puppet's heart.

For three winter months I saw him wither, reads Robin Underhill, every afternoon I would watch him from my bed, where I lay with my mother, feigning sleep, as he sat on the narrow verandah to syrup his wasting limbs in the winter sunlight, listening over and over to his favourite record:

> The day ends, in the land of sleep the same phantom
> And on the other shore, amid the golden corn
> The same spirit sings her distracting song –
> Oh come, those who would take this last boat with me
>   across the river.

It was the very last verse that was the most eerie, I would stand, washing drainslime off the much battered deuce ball at the creaky tubewell, and shiver as these last few strains sifted slowly through the darkness toward me:

He, who has not been blessed with the burden of flowers
He, whose crops have failed yet again
He, who can only laugh at his own tears
He, for whom the day is gone, and no light shines in the dark
It is he who sits in the shadows of the shore listening to her song.

And in the dining room, my mother would be waiting with whey and puffed rice that, in my hurry to be out on the streets with the boys, I had neglected to finish. Wash your hands, she would command softly, her eyes bright with tears, why not he rather than the neighbour's son, she surely wondered, what chord of steel separated our destinies, that he, with my name, and my face should waste away into the tropical silence, while I, I would thrive, would grow to manhood, and earn my keep as purveyor of promiscuous peptides, and I, rather than he, would one day, in a small South Calcutta garage, stumble upon the sternest secrets of life, why should his story fill one meagre paragraph, and mine more than can hold between these wide covers?

The boy returns from the water, wringing out his towel, he smiles and throws himself nearby onto the sand, are you a writing a story? he asks Yuri Sen.

You could call it that, says Yuri Sen, drawing swastikas in the sand.

I turn the page and read of my life: My brain was a plague of images without names, why call a cat a cat when it could as easily be called semicolon, a small voice would whisper within me whenever I tried to call the animal by a name, why not call chalk cheese and cheese chalk, a voice would tease, and I would be left standing in hapless confusion, pointing to the pudding that I wanted more of, while my mother vainly pleaded with me to articulate my wish. Perhaps this was why I later came to be so fond of chemicals, for they could be coded by simple combinations of letters, and yet each had also some ridiculous name that celebrated the joyful arbitrariness of such a scheme, Merck's Perhydrol, Oil of Wintergreen, Gentian Violet, Caustic Soda, Prussic Acid, names out of a post-lapsarian paradise, where appellatives only flirt with objects, and words simply celebrate their meanings rather than cleaving into them.

The boy rolls over onto his elbows, what is the moral of your story? he asks Yuri Sen.

Years later, reads Robin Underhill, I would reconstruct this holy space within a small private garage, but for then the highceilinged college laboratory was my temple, my lofty cathedral, the bench my high altar where daily I would offer my small sweet sacrifices, a burnt finger, a grazed knuckle, an acid-eaten cuff. But mine was the devotion of a humble priest, never was it the supple dedication of one who sought to raise himself to the level of the gods, never did I dare dream that I would brush my lips against their mightiest secrets, I was content to busy myself with smaller riddles, unravelling the composition of a subtle salt was my highest prayer, the simple fumes of a well synthesised acid my ultimate benediction.

Footsteps upon the sand, it is Anya, she walks past us, walks straight into the scalded roar of the sea, the boy lifts himself up and rushes in after her, he hovers by her as she walks deeper and deeper into the waters, battling against the capricious waves, a grim figure in white, and the boy nervously watching over her, ready to lunge if she should fall, she halts and balances herself against the angry waves, fixes her gaze upon the stark horizon, ponderous seawater mingles with the dampness of milk upon the thin cotton that drapes her breasts, come back please, the boy pleads, it is dangerous, the tide is coming in.

Three years ago, floating upon calm Midlantic waters, she had seen herself abducted by mermaids, taught to breathe through a thin tube attached to some floating device, they would keep her as a maid, an underwater Cinderalla, to comb dead seahorses out of their hair, and rustle up marvellous sea cucumber salads for their lunches, your true talents lie in cooking and sketching, her mother had told her, it is charcoal and garlic where you are at home, her mother had said to her, something as obdurate as language will only bruise your gentle fingers.

She turns around to face us, pushing away her salt-scorched hair from her eyes, walks slowly back, the boy following, she comes towards us over the sand, do you think my mother is dead? she asks me.

As if he would know any better than you, says Yuri Sen.

It's not even as if I care, she replies softly.

She picks up the open notebook that I have returned without comment to Yuri Sen, what have you been writing? she asks him.

I strayed too close to the stars, reads Anya aloud, and before I knew it I was stationed in a flat in Paddington, eating thick-cut marmalade for breakfast, and feeding antibiotics to lady-birds for a living, while in secret vaults men and women were brewing according to my instructions a most delectable primordial soup, the recipe of which I had stumbled upon entirely by accident, in a child's game of hide-and-seek turned into a manhunt, I who had set out in search of a warm fire and festal cheer had found myself guest at no ordinary banquet, but at a feast of magicians.

What is this? asks Anya.

Does it have a happy ending, asks the hotel boy hopefully, the story, does it end happily?

Take me home, says Yuri Sen.

His train arrives in Oxford, Robin Underhill shoves the sketchpad in the Marks & Spencer's bag, and walks out into the rainbled sunlight, he stops to buy a can of diet Lucozade, and begins to walk towards the city, the riverbanks are crowded with daffodils, he slips his empty can into the shopping bag and drops the whole load into the river, watches it sink into the green depths. Upon this very bridge Juan Gorrion had cursed him, someday Underhill I will ruin you, he had said, only half in jest, when he had discovered that Underhill had decided to run against him in the JCR elections, I will ruin you someday, he had repeated, shaking his hand after Underhill had won, I will come back into your life through paths that you never dreamed of, he had said, Juan Gorrion. That whole year he had kept a low profile in college, they said he was to be seen nightly with his Classics tutor, Percival Partridge, and his odd companions, at the Eagle and Child Halls, they wore black and smoked cigars, and avoided eating spinach in honour of Pythagoras, so it was rumoured, and also that Gorrion was applying for postgraduate positions in the States – where they respect passion – he had been heard to say. All that year he moved like a wounded ghost behind the curtains, it was not until winter that Robin Underhill would bump into him again, it was the last time he ever saw him, he was standing outside the college lodge gobbling candied hearts, thirty years ago, a bagful of little hearts that some woman had pointedly presented him, have some, Gorrion had said, thrusting the bag under Robin Underhill's nose, have some they're delicious, he had flung a cloud of candied hearts across the snow, welcome to the puppeteer's breakfast, he had said, welcome to the feast that starves the guest.

Epilogue

In a plush and solitary chair he waits, Yuri Sen, every evening, always reading, and yet never quite immersed, never quite with the earnest concentration that might be expected of one who is willing to engage in as private an act as reading, in this, the most public of places, the foyer of the Savoy, no, his nostrils twitch sullenly, fine firm nostrils, and one shoulder arches in anticipation of the delicate tap that is bound to come, like a dread changing of television channels, Mr Sen, your services are required, Mr Sen, to join the party, lest an unlucky thirteen be seated around one table, Yuri Sen, called upon to starve at another's feast, for while some graciously demand that he be fed as they, most are content for him to be discreetly served pork and potatoes, while they sculpt their uneaten caviare into corpuscular landscapes, Yuri Sen, the thirteenth man, the unlucky beggar, earning his living off the fat of chance.

How often will an unsuspecting group of diners find themselves a party of thirteen? he had laughed, months ago, when he had brought back the details of the job from the employment agency, look, he had pushed a paper pad of scribbles across to Anya, feeding the child, at the other end of the table. Oh, I wouldn't understand, she said, you forget I have not had an education. This is just simple probability, he had complained, anyway, take it from me that the chances of ending up with thirteen at a table are very small, and smaller still are the chances that they will care enough to pay for a stranger to sit among them to avoid being poisoned by the salmon mousse.

The first evening, he had settled himself in a quiet spot,

ordered a tall gin and tonic, and opened to the first page of *The Arabian Nights*, anticipating a thousand and one nights of uninterrupted entertainment, 'it is written in the chronicles of the Sassanian monarchs . . .', and there suddenly, before the end of the page, came the discreet tap, swallowtailed apologies, your services, Mr Sen, are most urgently required, a small private party has lost two guests to bad weather, their plane has been diverted to Manchester, just so you know, Mr Sen, in case you have to engage in small talk, though as a rule, they tend to ignore you, give the honorary status of death, see you as somewhat an ominous figure, if you know what I mean, after all they are never quite sure that they are really cheating fate.

Yuri Sen, burdening himself with others' bad luck, flinging his spilt salt over another man's shoulder, pushing mice away from laddered stockings, holding the black cat by its tail while others pass. Between three and seven, he is free, picks up the child from the crèche at half four, and walks back by the canal to their home on Edgware Road. The cream turrets fade, and their sootfaced abode eyes them balefully, as he tries to cross the road, they live above a greengrocer's, handy for tomatoes, which the child eats in vast quantities, tomatoes and honey, Anya mixes vitamins into the purée, the child will not eat anything else. She has painted her room white, very white, and even the old wooden cot where the child sleeps, she has painted glossy white, the room is mostly nursery, with her own narrow bed crouching shyly in the corner. She has not brought a man home with her yet, but someday soon she will, he knows, will she ask to use his room, he wonders, clear his broad bed of books, and find comfort, upon his naked duvet, in the arms of some penny youth, while he minds their child, takes it to the park to steal flowers for its mother, to feed the squirrels, it has not happened yet, but it will, he knows.

One afternoon, bringing the child home, he finds her upon a canalside bench, writing in a small notebook. I took the day off, she tells him, I had a bad headache this morning, she works in an antique shop on Portobello Road, I thought I would try and write some poetry, she says, staring into the dull waters. The child squats by a houseboat, and makes conversation with a tortoiseshell cat. He sits down besides Anya, and takes her hand, what strange peace is this that passes between us, he wonders, averting his eyes from her poetry, what is this thinveined peace that seeps from her small hand into mine, a duck and her young file neatly past, the childs hoots in delight, what is this limbless affection, he wonders, that rises to bind us, can it guide us, wonders Yuri Sen, to that great night, can it guide us, without agony, into that great night?

And I, many miles away, awaken one morning, aching with desire for you, and find, to my surprise, that I have made my peace with death. All day, I watch warily for the feeling to pass, death follows, arms quietly folded, he has done his duty here, he will rest now, for a time, we will play cards in the evenings, listen together to old fishermen's songs, until Esha's mother calls me to supper. We eat late, the two of us, wheaten flatbread that the cook has left warm under old towels, vegetable curries in small steel bowls, yoghurt after, slithery and alkaline upon my tongue, rather as I thought death might taste, once, long before he became a friend.

What is the true nature of loss, I wonder, that your flight into the wilderness of war should have left such a void, and Esha's violent death only a large rent in my being, badly stitched, but healed, its crooked lips pursed in contempt. Take care of her, you said, of your daughter, I did my best, she sends me photographs of herself and the child, her auburn curls running in rivers over her young arms, splashing over the child, and the slightest irritation upon her face, like that of the Dutch Madonna you sent me from Milan, the picture postcard painting of St Luke painting the holy family, kettle a-bubble in the gloaming, a placid bull at the Saint's feet, one horn a halo-stand, and the Madonna with the child upon her knee, faintly impatient, eager to return to her domestic duties, the patching and the darning, the making of matzoh balls, the peace that she had been wrenched from by her holiness, reluctant to see her beloved infant as the saviour of mankind. Like me perhaps she was not keen to burn her fingertips by reaching for the stars, or indeed for St Luke's halo, flung freely upon cowhorn, might she not have charred her holy fingers upon his halo, reaching as a good hostess to hand him his headgear, might she not have burned herself?

Take care of her, you had said to me, of your daughter, trembling sweet beside me, nursing within her the first flickering flames of a new life, unbeknownst to all. It would be years before your body would be found, sealed between cracks of strange stone, your canvas duffelbag squeezed beside your bones would be neatly delivered, its contents intact, to the small white flat in Edgware Road, where Anya would stumble, like a shipwreck, through the debris of your past, the guillotined photographs, the forsaken journals, the newspaper clippings of Esha's death, and the solemn notebook where you took notes for my autobiography. By the time Yuri Sen returns, at a quarter past midnight, she is sitting in the darkness, the child asleep upon her lap, her eyes are not coals as she says: I will finish his autobiography, I will fulfil my mother's promise, the notes are all there. He saved my child's life, I owe it to him.

There was once a magician, she tells the child as her bedtime story the following evening, there once was a magician, who wanted nothing more than to grow enough food to feed the world. And so he worked hard with his magic in his small dungeon (for he was a poor magician) until he made a small seed, which was like no other seed, but could fill a field with corn in an hour, fill the sea with fish in a day, fill the air with delicious fowl in a matter of minutes. He was about to creep off and try this wonderful seed in the quiet of the night, when his wife, who was a beautiful and very ambitious woman, caught him by the sleeve, and told him that if he did it all at night then in the morning no one would believe that it was all the magician's work – and we will be as poor as ever, complained his wife. And so reluctantly the magician agreed to wait until daytime, while word was sent out that such a deed was to be performed, and the crowds gathered in thousands, the king himself, all waiting to see this miracle. But when the time came for the magician to demonstrate the worth of this little seed, it was nowhere to be found, neither in the little casket where the magician had kept it all along, nor in the many folds of his clothes, nor within the dark strands of his magnificent hair, it was lost forever to mankind, the little seed that might have saved them all from hunger, was lost forever to this world.

And at this the child begins to weep, instead of tumbling into small sleep, she begins to wail, and Yuri Sen, sitting upon the sill, smoking a last cigarette before he heads to work, flings it out of the window and comes to comfort her, look how you have upset her, he accuses Anya, look at what you have done with your selfish tale.

She rushes away in blind grief to the bathroom, and when the child is asleep, he tiptoes in to find her staring into the stained depths of the tub, her chin a bruised blue upon the porcelain, someday I will fill it with hats, she tells him, I will fill this old tub with hats, divide its emptiness into felted cubbyholes.

And old shoes, says Yuri Sen.

And old shoes, she agrees, that wish they were hats.

Old shoes that wish they were hats, concedes Yuri Sen, and wring their laces in this agony.

He takes her hand, and again in the cheap diffractions of soft summer light, a gentle peace seals between them, what are these hollow tendrils of affection that bind us, wonders Yuri Sen, can it guide us, he wonders, into that gentle night, is it enough to propel us towards the ultimate lightness of being that will be mine long before it is hers, wonders Yuri Sen.

And I, many miles away, awaken to your daughter's request to once again encode some of my life, as it is now, and as it has been, the strange fitful gaps in the tale that her mother had attempted to erect and garnish with an ambition that was never mine. Would I agree to continue this bizarre exercise, she writes timidly, she has contacted Sir Percival Partridge, who is willing to pay her to finish the ancient project, whether out of nostalgia or simply pity, we would never know, feel free to scribble in Bengali, she advises, for Yuri Sen can act as an intermediary, to decipher and translate my communications. How can I refuse, why would I refuse, and yet what have I to tell her, my daily life is as colourless and eventless as it was ever meant to be, as it would always have been, if I had not been caught in the cat's cradle of a woman's selfless ambition, if I had not become victim to a woman's grand desire to possess the universe, and make me its lord.

Can I confess to her, my sweet Anya, that even on that second day of college, walking in the Chemistry lecture to fell the full tilt of Esha's eyes, that my heart had leapt not simply in unimagined happiness, but also in a great fear. For months I would lie, my face to the wall, wondering whether I would ever tire of my disbelief that she had chosen *me* as the object of her overwhelming affections, and reason that my disquiet rose too from this disbelief and not from the relentless force of her devotion. Unlike other girls I had known, she had never attempted to conceal the depth of her emotions, why would she need to, she was queen, I a mere subject, grateful, almost unbalanced by her favour, she did not need to manoeuvre me into desiring her, she was the ultimately desirable, the perfect being, who was I to turn away from her magnanimous passion?

Not that it ever crossed my mind that I might not love her, for my grainy lust took sharper shapes daily as I unearthed a new gesture, a new tilt to her head, a new movement of her eyes, feasting transparently upon her small graces, soft flourishes to a fantastic universe of communication that grew between us, as we discovered how snugly our hopes and dreams gloved into each other, except mine were empty relics of a deprived adolescence, while hers were the stuff of unblossomed galaxies, but this, like much else, we did not know then.

I was content to remain within her power, to fit quietly into the circles of steel that guarded her passions, but she would not have it so, for only in dominion could her independence flourish, when I stood first in the college examinations I could not help feeling that she had purposely scored low in Inorganic Chemistry, to let me have this honour, to tutor me in an arrogance that would close about her own desires, that they might deepen within its hold, rather than spread without horizons into a bleak and lonely future. For it was loneliness she feared most, that which was the least of my phantoms, I had spent my life seeking to be alone, she had spent her childhood in the company of silence.

It is this image that returns most often to me when I think of her: the ten-year-old child resting her cheek against the sunwarmed carcass of a rail carriage, grains of forest darkness slipping swiftly between her small fingers, that was a month of salt, Esha would tell us later, that was a month of petrified time, a mummified month, with each afternoon as slow crystals dissolving darkly upon her young tongue, she would wander the forest with her grandfather's rusty walking stick, stalk the small stretch of overgrown railway track, each day to revel in the mock discovery of the glorious wreck, the abandoned rail carriage, smooth with decay. And each morning she would wake to the whiteness of fierce sun, the sky a bed of dull salt, the starched clothes of her grandparents flapping mercilessly taut outside the window, and the acid smell of unformed paper heavy upon the back yard, the sad soapy smell that drenched the swimming pool where she would meet the officers' children, crammed into their thickwalled flats during the heat of midday, they would emerge in the afternoons to splash and swim and engage in a peculiar teenage frolic that she craved to be part of, the precocious young girl in her foreign swimsuit, the mill manager's granddaughter, they call her a little genius, she would never belong to their world.

In the evenings they would play badminton, in harsh floodlit patches, edged with laughing girls, and Esha would watch for a while before she was called in to supper with her grandparents, and then she was free to dream of the universe, of the woodpanelled library where the Creator drew his plans, handed them to his tall narrow-shouldered assistant, a man in a black cape carrying soap paper scented with bat milk, the thirteenth guest at every table, sprinkling salt into the gaps in the calendar, rubbing salt into the cracks of time, is it any wonder that she drew her breath so sharply when she first saw him, Yuri Sen.

She saw him by the rosebushes, a tall figure in black, the deep summer dusk not daring, it seemed to her, to settle upon his outlines, it was our first visit to Sir Percival's estate, he was keen to take me on a tour of the gardens before dark, and so we set off, almost as soon as we had arrived, Esha was too exhausted to join us, but later decided to bravely venture forth into the evening in the hopes of finding us, and came face to face instead, upon turning the first corner, with the spectre of Yuri Sen, wreathed in the scents of rotting paradise, for the air was heavy with the corruption of roses, that summer evening, when she first set eyes upon him, our Lucifer in limbo, Yuri Sen.

Where have I seen you before? she asked, before she could help it, have I not see you before?

I studied in Shantiniketan, he replied in Bengali. Only then did she realise that she had inadvertently posed her question in Bengali, to this stranger in this land of strangers, she had spoken, without thinking, in Bengali.

You are Bengali! she exclaimed.

In a manner of speaking, he replied. You must be the magician's wife, he said, pulling out a small white rabbit from under his black cloak and placing it carefully between two rosebushes.

My husband is a scientist, if that's what you mean, said Esha.

More a magician, from what I hear, said Yuri Sen.

You mock us, said Esha.

Welcome to the land of lonely people, said Yuri Sen, handing her an overripe rose, but try not to make it your home, he told her, wrapping his cloak tightly around him as a light breeze raised a mild turmoil of summer insects around their ankles.

We shall most definitely return after five years, said Esha. We come not in search of creature comforts, as many have done before us, we come not in search of a better life but only to fulfil a mission, which when it is complete, will release us to return.

And yet you will never escape, prophesied Yuri Sen.

You are quite a cynic, said Esha, annoyed, yet perplexed.

My mouth is my own graveyard, said Yuri Sen.

Three months after your remains are conveyed to your daughter, Yuri Sen spots Juan Gorrion's name in the papers, a quieter than usual evening at the Savoy, Yuri is reading through the major broadsheets a second time (serious reading, he has concluded, is not possible in this profession), suddenly he spies Gorrion's name, along with the details of his presidential candidature in his home country, to which the prodigal son has returned, after a long silence, an interminable diapause. Believed to have some years ago been killed in Eastern Europe, Gorrion has been living until recently under the pseudonym of 'Jack Swift' in Omaha, Nebraska, composing his memoirs, published last month under the title *A Possum's Apothegm*, and reported to be a fascinating read.

When he is sure no one is looking, Yuri Sen carefully rips out the small column, and puts it in his pocket, intending to show Anya, but when he returns, he finds her asleep, her cheek upon a blotted page of her notebook, where she has been faithfully transcribing tapes of her mother's conversation with an old woman in an orange cardigan, the last person in this world to hear Esha's voice. These she has discovered in an old trunk that you had left at Sir Percival's, which the old codger has sent her, he has conceived of a genuine interest in her mission, Sir

Percival Partridge, has even invited Anya and the child to come up for a weekend in the country. Should I accept? Anya had asked timidly, and Yuri Sen had replied, it's entirely up to you, what can I say?

The tapes, there are two of them, sixty minutes each, are largely grunts and chuckles and slurps and small talk, for you had cunningly concealed the tape recorder in your jacket, and excused yourself to visit the bathroom when the tape needed changing. Anya has waded assiduously through the inconsequential detail, *me daughter brings Chinese take-out whenever she comes to see me, gives me indigestion, does Chinese, but I can't tell 'er that, can I now?* reads Yuri Sen, halting at her elbow, he fingers the newspaper cutting in his pocket, he will never be able to bring himself to show it to her, instead he will slip in an envelope and print upon it my address, so that one summer morning I will receive the strange news that Juan Gorrion has surfaced intact from his mad journey, while you, who followed him into disaster, have returned a sack of bones.

That very afternoon, I make the long and arduous journey to the United States Information Services library in search of *A Possum's Apothegm*. They do not have it and are not keen to order it, who else would ever want to read it? they argue. I make my way through the pitted streets to the Grand Hotel arcade, and inquire at the trusty pavement shop where Esha and I almost maintained an account in the days when we came often to the heart of the city. The bookseller offers to attempt to procure a copy, never heard of the publishing house, he says, shaking his head suspiciously.

I have a new book on Derrida, he says to tempt me.

Not my racket, I tell him, smiling, I'm a scientist.

All eggs of the same basket, if you ask me, he says suddenly, your complex carbohydrates and their extended metaphors, all eggs of the same basket.

No need to make omelettes of them though, I reply self-consciously, and take my leave.

I walk on, past the faded cinema halls, the recently one-wayed streets, the brave façade of the Museum, finally I turn into Park Street, intending to buy some cakes from Flury's pâtisserie for Esha's mother. There was a time when we never returned from a trip to these parts without some small selection for her, éclairs and tartlets that she would consume with a quiet nostalgia, immersed in memories of her life in London in the fifties with her husband and son, both lost to her now, memories that she was somehow reluctant to share with us then, quite unlike my parents who spoke endlessly of the miseries of the War and the Partition, Esha's mother kept her reminiscences locked lightly against her lips, undispersed, intact, it was only after we were firmly bound for her beloved shores that she began to tell us a little of her life there as a young wife, complicitous practical details that only annoyed Esha – I'm sure things have changed now – she would say irritably to her mother – I'm sure little is as you remember it.

I pay for my pastries, and emerge again into the afternoon heat. There are no taxis to be seen, I walk wearily along the faded street, little here is as I remember it, gone are the grand façades, the curious shops, the honest decay of an underfed culture, instead all around me is cheap glass, tawdry windows glittering with the display of unfortunate imitations, I snatch myself away from the smirk of a pair of blue and yellow sneakers, run after a taxi, it stops but refuses to journey as far south as my home. I stand mopping sweat off my brow, take a step backwards and bump into three Anglo-Indian women, miserably thin, their dark limbs twisting like bits of wood out of their flowery frocks, watch where you're going, man, one of them screams as I tread upon her foot. I apologise and rush in through the dusty doors of an old antique shop, high-vaulted and cool, it is as welcoming as a temple, I close my eyes and inhale of an old communion: here the battles of wood and metal with the ravaging winds have been long resolved, here tarnish is grace, holy are the signatures of each lost orchestra of woodworms, the latticed scriptures of silverfish, felted between layers of time, I have come in search of old silver, I explain to the suspicious shopkeeper, he points a horny finger towards a half-closed door, and then, ignoring me, smoothes out a handkerchief upon his leathertop desk, and places upon it a peculiarly gnarled orange.

I feel obliged to explore beyond the mysterious door, and pushing it gently open, enter an alkaline darkness, my groping hands touch a pile of ancient betelnutcrackers, caked in thick dust. Pure silver, a voice assures me, in a crack of light from the unpatched ceiling an Oriental face appears, heavy with make-up, I can hardly see anything, I complain to the apparition. You will get used to it, she says calmly, as if I have been condemned to spend the rest of my life within this bizarre mausoleum, this Aladdin's cave, as perhaps she has been, exiled amid ruined silver, perhaps she will only be released when it is all sold, perhaps she sleeps upon the mess of rags in the corner, taking shape now as my eyes accustom themselves to the gloom, this fantastic darkness, speared by lightshafts from the broken ceiling. Does she sleep then upon the pile of old blankets in the corner, each morning wipe a pockmarked plate to study her face, ink her slit eyes with black oxides of silver, and smear her cheeks with the red oxides of iron, rust and tarnish, the devil's true palate, perhaps she has been enslaved by the cruel patron, promised her freedom upon turning these grimy piles to sparkling silver. I am looking for a small silver frame, I tell her, a small silver frame.

Like this? she asks hopefully, emptying a shoebox onto a smooth surface that I later recognise as a glass countertop. Frames of all shapes and sizes tumble out, like pieces of an open-ended jigsaw. I feel I am violating the very fabric of time as I extract from among them a small simple wreath, blackened beyond recognition, just a good wash with ordinary soap will restore it to its former splendour, the woman assures, she names a fabulous price, it belonged to Maria Chapusettin, the wife of Warren Hastings, she claims, it once held her portrait, painted by her first husband, for she was the wife of a German miniaturist before she married Warren Hastings. Naturally she disposed of such relics very rapidly and discreetly at the time, for two hundred years it has languished in anonymity, my seductress sighs, I am captivated by this fabrication, begin to rake my pockets for cash, we take credit cards, she tells me discreetly, with a toothless smile.

May I never rest my head again upon a shoulder that does not quiver but a little under a patina of untruths, let my palate never be soothed but by the grazings of tongues thick with secrets, let my lust never be quickened but by the sheen of deception upon trembling eyes, may you all thread my tale with intoxicating inexactitudes, may the glass of my coffin sweat beads of imposture, may a tissue of lies be my shimmering shroud.

I emerge from the shop, blinking in the strong sunlight, chase after a few taxicabs, and find myself at the heavy crossroads, the crowds thickening around me as the afternoon wears on, perhaps I should try the underground railway, I muse, they tell me it is fast, and not always crowded, I approach the yawning entrance tentatively, find myself walking slowly down the marbled stairs, I sense a strange excitement within me, as the great king Yudhisthir might have felt, I flatter myself, upon being led into a brief journey through hell, in atonement for the one white lie he had ever told in his life, the price of one lie, a cursory sojourn of hell (where his brothers roasted), to preface an eternity in heaven. I feel his heart might have quickened as mine does now, are these the wages of the sum of my sins, then, a short ride on the Calcutta Metro from Park Street to Tollygunge, facing a wall of pallid, listless, exhausted strangers, these are not my people, I say to myself, I do not know these people, where have they come from, who are they?

Suddenly I recognise in the corner, clad in baggy trousers, a thin moustache wisping upon his upper lip, my nephew, Tapan, my brother's son, grown suddenly older in the three months since I saw him last, why do you never visit us? he asks me, I will, I will, I promise, where are you off to, then? Coaching classes on Southern Avenue, he answers, wearily.

They came to see his sister yesterday, he tells me.

Who came to see her? I ask.

The parents of a prospective groom, of course, he replies, dismayed by my confusion, what else might I mean?

But she is only eighteen, I protest.

Nineteen, he corrects me.

Nineteen, then.

Mother says she will never get through her BA, my nephew says, might as well get her married.

This is absurd, I tell him, this why I never visit you, I would only end up arguing with your father.

He is silent, stares dully out of the window at the walls streaking by. My mind is a kaleidoscope of images, peaceful memories, my niece, little Papiya, a head full of curls, curled up between myself and Esha on winter afternoons, Esha singing her to sleep with old folk songs, I remember how she would dance for us, and more shyly in front of our friends. We loved to show her off, little Papiya, born two months premature in a long hot summer, would she live, I would tremblingly wonder, bent over my college texts on sticky breathless afternoons, while the boy next door played over and over again the same album, *no one knows what it's like to be the bad man, to be the sad man, behind blue eyes.* The only respite from this music came with power cuts, which were frequent enough, the fans would come to a dull halt, and I would slam my books shut in frustration, spread a bamboo mat upon the floor and court a syrupy sleep, will she live, I would wonder, what sacrifice of mine will it take for her to live?

So what did they think of her? I ask Tapan gently.

He smiles, I have to get off here, he says, come and see us soon.

Another stop and we reach the end of the line, I stumble into eerie sunlight, find a rickshaw to take me home, set my battered box of cakes upon the seat next to me, mop my forehead with my handkerchief, and lift the creaky hood to shield me from the late afternoon sun. Esha's mother is delighted with the cakes, I haven't had an éclair in years, she says, at least ten years, I will make some special Darjeeling tea, she declares, rushing into the kitchen.

I head for the bathroom to take a shower, but the overhead tank has basked all afternoon in the fierce sun, the water is warm and unsatisfying, I take a full bucket that stands in the corner and pour the cooler bucket water over my head. Finally refreshed, I emerge and dress in my house robes, white cotton pantaloons, and a loose white *punjabi* shirt, I examine my new silver frame, and attempt to restore its shine with an old toothbrush and some soap, by which it does acquire some semblance of silver, I dry it and trim a black and white photograph of Anya and the child to fit within it, I place it within a small alcove where Esha kept her few powders and potions, a shrine-like space built into the wall, it now holds a small brass vase with some withered flowers which I push to one side to make room for the photograph, experiment with where exactly to place it until Esha's mother calls me to tea.

My fondest memory of England, she says, through a mouthful of choux pastry, my sweetest memory is of the three of us, Esha's father, her brother and myself, huddled in our chairs on some damp afternoon, listening to scratchy records of Tagore songs, the music strangely dissonant with the winter gloom, I would watch the smoke rise from the low chimneys, and pray to the Lord to bless my happiness, to bless my family, to bless my people in the land we had never really left behind.

One morning she is woken by her mother, scrubbed clean in the cracked bath, and dressed in a blue cotton frock, neat white socks, and her best shoes, sent to kiss Yuri goodbye, who accepts her embrace with unusual indifference and returns to his newspaper, enjoy yourselves, he says with sarcasm, that she does not recognise, simply senses an oddness, and a curious determination on her mother's face, as she hauls her downstairs. They take the underground to Paddington, where the bear came from, her mother tells her, but was he real, Paddington Bear, she asks, her friends have laughed at her for thinking him real, so that she knows he must not be, and yet believes he is, and wonders how she can believe and not believe at the same time, and knows that what she would really like is to meet his cousin, also come all the way from Peru, keep him in their Edgware Road flat, keep him to play with and to help with her sums, keep him her secret, so that when her friends laughed at her for believing that Paddington Bear was real, she could smile, secretly smile, save some marmalade pudding from school dinner to take back to him, her bear, waiting for her in her Edgware Road flat, waiting for her to come home to tea.

Sir Percival is at the station to meet them, dressed in a blue linen suit and a goldenrod shirt, he also wears a blue-banded yellow hat, which he gives her to hold, as it threatens to fly off in the opentop car. She puts it over her head, holding tight its brim, and breathes in its seashell dark, when suddenly a truant wind whips it from her clutch, and Blake has to stop the car and chase after it, her mother scolds her for her carelessnes, but Sir Percival laughs, it's just a silly hat, Anya, he says, let the child be.

Before lunch, they walk in the gardens, to work up an appetite, Sir Percival says, as if she isn't dying already of hunger. We have not had many flowers this year, Sir Percival complains, she stoops to follow the track of a brilliantly coloured caterpillar, and discovers a pale pink flower, which she promptly picks and proudly presents to her mother, who takes it but chides her, you must not pick other people's flowers, her mother tells her.

Yuri is forever teaching her these terrible habits, Anya complains to Sir Percival, they never go for a walk in the park without returning with a large bouquet, it's embarrassing, I really don't know what to do.

But Sir Percival only throws back his head and laughs, so Yuri is teaching her to steal park flowers, he says.

And what else I wonder at times, Anya says with a sigh.

Time for lunch, says Sir Percival, crushing a beetle under his heel.

Long ago he had helped pin flowers in her hair, woven daisies into her long copper tresses, she wore a simple tunic, and flowers in her hair, young Anya, while we struggled with our elaborate costumes for our fancy-dress luncheon, you begowned and jewelled, your feet already starting to bleed within your glass slippers, you were Cinderalla, and Yuri Sen, some fantastic beast, straight out of Hieronymus Bosch, I helped him strap on his great and flimsy wings. I was going as Sir Percival, and Sir Percival as myself, I waited for him to give up his watch chain, but he was pinning flowers in Anya's hair, wholly mesmerised, while she stared out into the garden, watched the fickle morning light brushing the wet flowerbeds, the lawns, the empty swimming pool, thick with dead leaves, she saw the narrow clouds rushing away from her, and suddenly caught her breath, Anya, in first full moon, *your evenings heave with sombre sweet dreams, the screams of suddenly woken nestlings spasm through your slender womanhood, the flower smells of the first rains stain your sleep, and within your breast rise the murmurings of an old forest, from time to time an unknown sadness smothers the corners of your new horizons, your eyes swell with tears*, these words of the Poet came then to my mind, many years ago, for we had all sensed the intoxications of her new awakening, Sir Percival frantically pinning flowers in her hair, you casting faintly disapproving glances in her direction, irritated yourself by my helpless devotion, stale now upon your tongue, staler still against your daughter's fresh full bloom. We were all a little drunk with her youth that day, Sir Percival plaiting daisies into her hair, my mind steeped in the delicate eroticism of Tagore's paean to maidenhood, and by the washbasin, trying desperately to ward off her tender lust by swabbing his face with green ink, the curious object of her nascent desires, Yuri Sen.

At lunch, they eat larks on toast, and she drinks lemonade while her mother and Sir Percival pop champagne, they eat caviare, which she finds too salty, and wild mushrooms with garlic butter, a huge salmon arrives, poached in Sauterne, the piece that she is served has too many bones, and her mother is too merry to notice. They open a second bottle of champagne, her mother and Sir Percival keep giggling and wiping their eyes. She pushes the salmon around her plate, it has a funny strong smell anyway, she is grateful when Blake places before her a large bowl of jelly and custard, which she attacks with glee, while her mother and Sir Percival eat kumquats and duck liver, she gobbles green jelly, and then slips under the table to a make-believe world between the snowy flaps of white linen, her mother's gentle knees, quivering with laughter, and Sir Percival's squat legs, planted wide apart, their legs are gateways to great kingdoms, guarded by goblins, she decides, and before she can decide who might venture through these strange gates, she falls into a custard-thick sleep. When she wakes, she finds herself alone, she crawls out from under the table, the remains of lunch are still strewn upon the table, a few bees humming quietly above the carnage, and through the French windows she can see her mother, stretched out upon a flowery sofa, sound asleep. She creeps out into the garden, follows a path through the parched rosebushes to a strange structure, its bottom half opaque glass, and top half brick, like an inverted greenhouse. There are rusty stairs that she climbs, pushes open the door, and finds herself in the apartment where Yuri Sen had spent seven years of his life, it is bare beyond all comprehension, for Sir Percival had burnt all his things. The floors, she notices with a shock, are glass, beneath her feet is the ruin of an aviary, branches bleached white with silence, cobwebs shot with birdseed hang like abandoned wedding veils, birdfeathers lie in small dry piles upon the floor. The child feels a hot fear gather within her, she runs out of the room, down the rickety stairs, through the sinister rose garden, back into the house, her mother is still sleeping, her face against the cushions, she sits for a while on the floor beside her, until her fear drains away, leaving her cool and calm, ready for a new adventure.

This time she chooses to wander further into the house, past the strange dusty tapestries in the hall, and down the stairs into the kitchen, where she finds herself face to face with a large black-haired woman, dusting the kitchen table with a goose-wing, her coarse hands rimmed with flour. Are you hungry, child? she asks her, the afternoon light slants in through the high basement windows, I can make you some drop scones, the woman says to her, sit down now, here, sit here. She obeys almost in a trance, sits quietly, absorbing the comforting play of light and shade upon the tiled flor, and the wideness of time in the ticking of two clocks, placed side by side upon the mantelpiece. One by one the scones arrive, warm and tender in melting cream and clover honey, she is given a glass of milk to drink, here is love as she has never known it, nor will ever know again.

And many miles away, while searching idly through a desk drawer for Sellotape, I suddenly close my forefinger and thumb about a small copper earstud, companion I surmise swiftly to the very article that had many years ago wrought magic and mayhem in my laboratory, when it had dropped accidentally from Esha's ear into the unholy brine. I weigh the priceless

object on my palm, let it roll gently back and forth between the
seams of my fate, I could analyse it, this strange hybrid metal, I
could subject it to chemical analysis, and the whole world
would again be at my feet. But behind my shoulder, death
frowns, death my new companion, clutches the chessboard to
his chest and frowns, and I know then that to unravel the
proportions of elements within this miraculous amalgam would
be to lose my peace with death, I know then that to unlock the
secrets of this fabulous alloy would be a sin beyond all pardon, I
set about preparing my laboratory for my final and very private
performance of turning gold into grass.

The child wipes the milk fringe off her upper lip, and slides
contented off her chair, offers the woman a shy smile of
gratitude, and climbs back up into the hallway, takes the great
stairs to the upper floor, walks down a long corridor peeping
into any room whose door she finds ajar, in one she finds Sir
Percival, sitting with his back to her at a window, listening to
Beethoven's Spring Sonata, music that makes her feel strangely
hopeful that some adventure is about to befall her, she treads
softly away, resumes her exploration of the rest of the house,
and finds herself eventually in a room full of old toys, arranged
neatly upon shelves, motheaten teddy bears, earless rabbits,
bandaged dolls, rusty train sets, old wooden blocks, a velvet
snail, and inside an empty closet beside the shelves, two
hundred strange names, pencilled on the inside of the doors.
Yuri Sen has told her of a time when in this great house two
hundred children came to stay, the great tubs of soup were
made to feed them, and a great many eggs broken to make them
all one large omelette, and for dinner, a large giraffe's neck,
roasted and laid out upon a long table, so that the two hundred
might eat to their content, for they were poor starving wretches,
he had told her, refugee children from a land ravaged by war.
She tries to read the names that climb the length of the doors,
and spies suddenly in the corner of the closet a ragged child, did
they leave you behind? she asks him, were you left behind,

then? He nods numbly, looks at her imploringly, and stretches out a skinny hand. She takes his small cold fingers in her hand, and climbs over a basket of wooden apples to sit beside him, does no one know about you? she asks. He nods again, silently. Poor boy, she says to him, I will hold you now, we will be friends.

We are having a late cup of tea when the doorbell rings, it is Esha's cousin Nilima, she has been all day at a Women Schoolteachers' Association meeting, for which she has come down all the way from Darjeeling. It is being held in a small school in Ranikuthi, she explains, not very far from our home, I thought I would drop by, she says, fanning her large face with the fantail of her sari. You must stay with us, Esha's mother implores. But they have made perfectly adequate arrange-ments for us at the school, Nilima protests. Stay with us just this night, Esha's mother pleads, she has been starved for so long of the company of female relatives, I see an unusual longing on her face, do stay, I say to Nilima, just this night. Nilima is flattered, for I have never expressed a fondness for her company, this self-righteous spinsterish cousin of Esha's, teacher of Physics at a convent school near Darjeeling. During the pujas we would often escape to her little flat in the hills, while she, mercifully, came down to Calcutta to spend her holidays with her mother, now many years dead. For the few days that we overlapped, she would drive me to despair with her constant moralising, I would at every opportunity excuse myself and go for a walk, wander all afternoon through the hillside mists, dead water dripping around me from the stormsuckled Japanese Cedars, and the Kanchenjunga, now clear and cold in the distance, now vanished behind thick veils of cloud, elusive, immutable, I would return disdained by the great mountains, humble and human, only to have my profound state of grace destroyed by this woman's loathly chatter. Do stay, I beg of her today, in consideration for Esha's mother, do stay this one night, I request her, and taken aback by this abrupt show of goodwill, she accepts.

Almost immediately I excuse myself, return to the garage, where I have already built the precarious hive of glass that will support my last miracle, an act that will destroy as it creates. I roll up the sleeves of my *punjabi* shirt and set about adding the final touches to the stage of my final communion with the devil.

Anya dreams that a mysterious captor has covered her body in the finest of Braille, tattooed every inch of her in this inscrutable tongue while she has slept, drugged by violets. For a week he has worked, madly, without sleep, written on her body in an unknown language, wrapped her in this invisible lace, for looking at her you would not know how she was inscribed, holding her even you would not feel the precious weight of these words, only the lightest and lovingmost of touches would yield this vast secret, these thinly etched vowels, the soft swell of each consonant, only the most patient of fingers would know. She knows it will take her years to master this language, she must devote herself to learning Braille, until she is confident that she will understand every word of what has been written on her body by a stranger, long-departed, never seen again. And all this while she will fear every scar, every small blemish that might wipe away his art, she will shield her skin as she might shield her soul, lest some careless encounter with a rusty nail should besmirch his message, splinter his poetry, Blake taps her softly, clears his throat and announces a phone call for her. Ribbons of writing still staircased around her gullet, she makes her way to the telephone, it is Yuri Sen, you are not back yet, he remonstrates, why aren't you back yet?

I fell asleep, she yawns, we had too much champagne at lunch.

Yuri Sen snorts. I see he has kept his old habits, he says of Sir Percival.

We will take the next train, says Anya.

I was worrying about you, Yuri Sen tells her.

Don't you have to go to work? Anya asks with another yawn.

I'm calling from work, he replies.

Oh, says Anya.

So how was it anyway? asks Yuri Sen.

Just perfect, says Anya, I really needed it, the kid really needed it, we went for a walk before lunch, and she picked a flower for me . . .

I have to go, says Yuri Sen.

Indeed he does, for white gloves are beckoning, the Thaumaturgical Society of Walthamstow are missing their fourteenth and fifteenth members, a middle-aged magician couple by the name of Frye, he will learn later, they have quarrelled, and turned each other into frogs, their fellow necromancers surmise, leaving them an unlucky party of thirteen, so that Yuri Sen is summoned to avert the misfortune that may particularly befall a gathering of thirteen wizards, he sits among them, silently eating his peas and lamb, while they punctuate their sombre courses with tricks and jugglery, Yuri Sen finds himself an unwilling subject of their hypnoses, at one point the room seems to disappear, and they are suddenly suspended, table and all, in endless intergalactic space, heavily encrusted with stars, to outdo this another magician makes them hang from the ceiling, the indifference of the other diners is all he has to confirm that these are all illusions, but then, thinks Yuri Sen, with the English, who can tell?

Many miles away, Esha's mother, making up a bed for our unexpected visitor, finds a graveyard of capsules between the mattresses upon the bed where he had slept and suffered, Yuri Sen, his lungs caked in filth, suspicious of my ministrations, spitting out his antibiotics and stuffing them beneath his overmattress for Esha's mother to find many years later, a field of broken soldiers, languishing upon coir.

She calls me to come and see this, but I am locked away in the garage, brewing a strange mixture that will yield chlorophyll upon contact with the truant earstud, but simultaneously dissolve the precious catalyst, erase this act from history in one last burst of original autolytic sin. He is still in his laboratory, Nilima tells Esha's mother, he has been there all evening, the old woman mutters, what on earth is he up to, I wonder.

Where is the child, wonders Anya, where in this wide house can she be? She hunts in the garden, softly sinister in the late light of a summer evening, still half in dream Anya hunts for her daughter, parting bushes, calling her name, she looks in the stables, graced now by a single lonely horse, the ageing Parsifal, the other stalls are empty, and she is not there, I cannot find her, she says to Blake, waiting on the patio with a tea tray, I simply cannot find her.

He sets down the tea tray, she picks up a small cucumber sandwich and absently eats it, we will look in the house, says Blake.

You take the upstairs, I will search downstairs, suggests Blake, I know she is not in the kitchen.

Yuri didn't want us to come, he knew something bad would happen, says Anya, breaking down suddenly into trembling sobs.

She will be found, says Blake grimly.

The devil take him, thinks Blake, the devil take him, Yuri Sen.

Their meal is entirely black, painstakingly copied from Perec's *Life: A User's Manual*: caviare, squid cooked in its own ink, saddle of baby Cumberland boar, truffle salad and blueberry cheesecake, although for Yuri Sen it is peas and mush, and leftover lamb, for the Thaumaturgical Society acknowledge his presence only by including him in their bizarre acts – Yuri Sen has to endure successively the sensations of his fingers turning into small snakes, flowers growing inside his mouth, rabbits popping out of his ears, and a multitude of imps and leprechauns scuttling about, moving his wineglass as he reaches for it, combing their hair with his forks, playing frisbee with his after-dinner mints, Yuri Sen, a sorry beggar at this council of magicians, watching his fate dissolve into a pile of salt.

Anya wanders from room to room, each darker and emptier than the other, the child's name stuck in her throat like a broken butterfly, struggling to take wing, her mind fills with the kisses of a black-haired youth who had worked for a while in a neighbouring shop selling stained glass. He had walked back with her from Portobello Road one day after weeks of silent watching, he had kissed her passionately by the canal, under the M40 bridge, cars and trucks roaring over them, he had linked her lips with an unknown violence that she tasted sweet all night, and in the morning when she woke, lay long in the bath, scraping her limbs, ironed a new summer frock to wear, and put on her mother's pearl earrings, but he was not at work, nor ever seen again, her mind fills with his kisses, these are my just deserts, she wonders bitterly, to have lost my child to this unfathomable mansion, to have lost my child to this wild English summer, this is my punishment.

She walks in a daze into a roomful of toys that she recognises as the many unloved beasts and objects that had arrived second-hand for the refugee children to play with, long ago. They had not been allowed to take the toys with them when they were herded back to their own country. The closet door is open, and there, praise the heavens, is the child, curled asleep around a laundry bag, Anya flings back the doors to wake her, and notices a ladder of names pencilled down each side, the two hundred refugee children that Juan Gorrion had followed to their deaths, leaving a telephone number under your tooth-glass, so that you might follow him, leaving me to finish my own tale, before it was barely begun.

I cradle the copper earstud in my palm, blowing gently upon it, as the glass cauldrons steam and shudder in anticipation of my terrible deed. I place my cheek upon my palm, and feel the ribbed sharpness against my flesh, years ago I had bought Esha the pair at the winter fair in Shantiniketan, we were still students then, it may have been my first present to her, let me buy it for you, I had suggested, praying that I would have enough money, in fact I had to borrow money later from a fellow student to cover my expenses, but my rash act had secured me the tenderest of smiles from Esha, and that evening as we all sat in a circle and sang songs, she looked once at me, then dipped her eyes and sang, *is it only the rising wave that seals the rhythm of the ocean, what of the tune of the wave that falls?* I felt as if my whole being would collapse in this concentration of joy, I felt as if my soul would never be but one with hers, that nothing would ever crush this knot of hardening stone, she lifted her face, her eyes closed, she sang, *is spring merely a carnival of flowers?*

I turn around hearing a sound behind me, it is Nilima, come to call me to dinner. It is nearly midnight, she says, we had completely lost track of time, talking of old times, she explains smugly, aren't you hungry?

I will be another few minutes, I tell her.

What are you doing, anyway? she asks, sniffing the curious air.

It's too complicated to explain, I say curtly.

I do have a Master's degree in Physics, you know, she answers, offended, I may just be able to understand your experiment if you explain it carefully enough.

It's not an experiment, I say.

What is it then? she demands.

I will be about ten minutes, I tell her firmly.

You are behaving as if you are about to commit some heinous crime, she says.

I ignore this statement, hoping she will simply leave.

You look like a ghost, she continues.

Another silence, short and merciless.

You must miss her, she says suddenly, I remember how the two of you were always in this garage, Esha agonising over some arcane corollary while you pottered around at the bench, she sighs and wipes a tear from her eye.

Do you miss her? she asks, accusingly.

I will be another few minutes, I say, through clenched teeth.

Suit yourself, she says, and finally leaves, I get up and bolt the door, check the preparation with a thermometer, and take the earstud finally between my fingers, and then, like the village child throwing into the fetid pond his dead sister's stolen necklace, I toss the truant earstud into the beaker, and watch as it tosses and gasps, sets the liquid into spasm, churns green from nothingness, and then is swallowed by the primordial broth.

> *You cast him as a beggar in your great game*
> *The skies trembled with laughter*
> *Many roads has he travelled, knocking on many doors*
> *Filling his beggar's bowl with scraps*
> *Only so that you might steal his alms*
> *He thought he would forever remain a beggar in this life*
> *He thought he would be a beggar beyond death*
> *And when at the end of his journeys*
> *He came fearfully to your door*
> *You received him with your own garland of flowers.*

Years from now, Robin Underhill will take his grandchild on a stolen afternoon to the Royal Ballet, how excited she will be, tripping with eager laughter as her mother fixes ribbons in her hair, small and snug her chattering fingers in his hand, they will climb their way to their seats, and there she will find, poor soul, that she cannot see, for Robin Underhill will have bought not quite the cheapest of seats, but still flung far into the cruel arc of the balconies, she will find her view badly sliced by bands of old darkness, but the audience will be sympathetic, she will watch *Giselle* with her chin on the balcony, between the kind knees of a cauliflowered matron, and Robin Underhill, in the shadows, will wish he were dead.